This book is a work of fiction.

LADY RISES

Renee Bernard

Cover Design by Cora Graphics.

*This book is dedicated to Megan Bamford. Because there has never been a bigger heart, a kinder soul or a sweeter friend. And when I needed it most, she was there. With a generous spirit, an infectious laugh and sparkling dragons to make me believe in myself again.*

*And to Andrew Bamford. Because every heroine needs a hero and I still tell everyone how incredible it is to see you with Megan and to see real chivalry and love in action. You inspire me, too.*

*And to my girls who are growing too fast.*

*And my beloved husband who will never grow up too fast (which is one of his many appealing qualities).*

## Acknowledgments

I know. We just did this a book ago and you're thinking, "My God, how many people can one woman thank?" The answer is that if I took the time to acknowledge everyone who had an oar in the water and was keeping my little raft afloat, we'd certainly hit a bigger page count. Who doesn't love a bigger page count?

But I will do my best to keep it brief. After all, the last book ended with a bit of a cliff-hanger and I'm sure most people are really anxious to simply get on with it.

I'm going to thank my Street Team again. Because they deserve it. Bernard's Bombshells are amazing and I want to thank each and every one of you for all the time and effort you've put into getting things off the ground. Ladies. I owe you a drink, or two, or several.

And no book happens without Lindsey Ross, my incredible friend and Executive Assistant/Online Goddess. Because only Lindsey lets my characters call her up and complain when things aren't going well and only Lindsey lets Ashe text her.

I have to thank Maire Claremont for providing more than a cover quote. When you admire another author's work, it's always humbling when they turn out to be one of the nicest human beings you've ever met. And to Delilah Marvelle who also generously gave me more than a quote but also a huge shot in the arm when I needed it. Thank you, Ladies!

And Last but Never Least, Mom. We built memories together with the girls this summer and I loved that. You are still my best friend in the world. No matter what comes, it's you and me. I wouldn't have it any other way.

# Lady Rises

## Renee Bernard

*"It is the passions you bury alive deep in your past that haunt you the longest and greet you at the grave." –A.R. Crimson*

Prologue

Kent, 1866

Phillip stumbled up the stone steps of Oakwell Manor, his legs numb from the pace of his ride. His clothing was sodden and his coat felt like it was woven from iced iron as it swung against him. He pounded on the door, caught in the furious storm of his emotions.

Walters opened the door with an expression of mild surprise but was no match for Phillip's momentum. He was past the man before he'd spoken a single word, marching toward the beckoning light in the ground floor study.

"Trent!" he roared before he'd crossed the threshold. "Trent! You son of a bitch!"

The Earl leaned back in his chair and calmly set down his book. "Warrick!" he said cheerfully. "Not on your honeymoon?"

"You bastard! You well know that I am not!" Phillip ran a hand through his wet hair to pull it off his face. "You know more than anyone!"

"Yes, that is probably true." Trent was all smiles. "Did you come by for enlightenment?"

For one fleeting breath, Phillip nearly launched at the smug figure seated before the fire, his hands curling into claws prepared to tear the earl's throat out—but god, more than the satisfaction of murder, he desperately wanted to understand why his life had taken such a horrifying turn. "Yes. Enlighten me, old friend."

"I once promised to be your mentor, did I not? But I failed you, dear boy. You crossed me long ago and I neglected to punish you. Let's just say, that I vowed to set things right."

"I...crossed you? How?" Phillip's breath caught in his throat. "Long ago? That courtesan? Are you—is it even possible?"

"I assure you, it is more than possible. It is a certainty. You had the audacity to mount another man's prized mare without so much as a by your leave, Warrick." Trent's cheery demeanor began to fall away. "You made a mockery of me! But you've got the bitter end of it now."

"That was years ago! You—said you'd forgiven all!"

"A bit of a lie, that. I apologize."

"So all of it? Raven was—all of this was some kind of scheme to destroy me in payment for tupping a slut you once bought a few dresses for?"

"I had that slut's keeping!" Geoffrey screamed and then went as still as stone. "No need to revisit that now. But how is your bride?"

"What do you mean how is my bride? I've come here to fetch her! Tell her to come down, Trent!"

Geoffrey's mouth fell open, his eyes alight with excitement, as he left his chair at last. "Tell me. Tell me what happened when you read my letter, Phillip. Tell me every detail and I will do what I can."

Phillip could taste ashes in his mouth at the sick and strange turns in their conversation. But he wanted Raven. "What is there to tell? I read the letter while we were still in the carriage en route to Gretna Green."

"Impatient boy! Did I not write on the envelope that you were to wait until after your marriage?"

"That? *That* is your complaint now?" Phillip had to clench his jaw and count to three before he could continue. "Raven was asleep and I found the note in my pocket. I didn't think it would make any difference… But it made all the difference, didn't it?"

"You didn't make your wedding vows?"

Phillip pressed a hand to his eyes, the grip of a headache starting to clamp down. "We weren't in any hurry. We'd stopped along the way and…I never thought to rush."

"The letter."

"Yes! I read it! I was bored and it was pouring rain to make for slow going and I read the damned thing!" Phillip dropped his hand, fury carrying him past the pain. "It was an ugly scene, sir! I woke her and threw her from the carriage! I ordered the driver to ride on and had every intention of never turning back!"

"Brilliant!"

"Was it? The carriage barely made it to the next hamlet before the mud became too much and the roads impassable. I was drinking at a roadside inn and cursing both of you to the fiery pits of Hell when it—occurred to me that I'd made a mistake."

"Only one?" Trent prodded with a laugh.

"Raven is mine. The lack of dowry stings but money can be made, sir. If there is one lesson you did convey before descending into madness, it was that one. As for the rest of her villainy, I…" Phillip swallowed hard. Here was the harder hurdle. His instincts said that Raven was an innocent when he'd taken her that first time, and he'd have sworn her maidenly barrier was not contrived with theatrics. But the vile flatness of the language the earl had used; the vague threat that every male servant inside this hall was even now laughing at him behind his back because they'd had her in every room of Oakwell Manor… Phillip started to choke on the bile that rose up his throat. "It is between us. I will attend to her failings and if I have to keep her under lock and key, then so be it. Tell her to come down."

"And my promise to notify the papers?"

"By all means," Phillip countered. "Of course, you'll have to include that she was *your* ward and under your supervision. The implications will be that you approved. Approved of every misstep and may have even encouraged it. I fail to see how your reputation is not also forfeit, so by all means. Contact the reporters. I'm sure they will have all manner of questions about how to raise a vile slut as one would a house cat."

Trent nodded. "Good point and one I hadn't considered. Good man! Oh, well. I will savor my victory in private then." Geoffrey brushed off his hands. "Thank you for stopping by. I'm sorry I can't offer you a room but you have so much to do, sir."

"Yes. Keep your petty revenge, you piece of shit. Now, Raven. Tell her to come down," Phillip repeated, a new chilling fear snaking up his spine. "The weather delayed my return but when she wasn't…She'd abandoned all her things but I know she would have found her way back home."

Geoffrey tugged on the bell pull. "She is not here."

"She has to be here."

The earl smiled. "No. Don't be a simpleton. A woman abandoned in a rainstorm by the side of the road with dark fast approaching? Use your imagination, boy. Go on. What do you suppose can have happened to your Raven by now?"

"God. No." In his glorious upset, he'd seized only on the one outcome. She'd thrown a fit by the side of the road, dumped out her trunks in a temper and then marched homeward until securing transportation of her own so that she could return to the welcoming arms of her nefarious guardian and his praise for her conquest.

But now...his imagination achieved a dozen horrifying scenarios in the space of a single heartbeat and Phillip staggered back as if the earl had struck him in his midsection with an andiron.

Trent clapped his hands in malicious glee. "Look on the bright side, baron. Your whore has given you a gift and freed you of worry. Death is a quick solution and she's either drowned in a fen, succumbed to the cold of exposure or actively hung herself from the first obliging tree she could find." The earl shook his head. "It amazes me how women are so resourceful!"

"I murdered her," Phillip whispered.

Strong hands began to seize his arms and Phillip's misery was compounded by the humiliation of realizing he was about to be forced from the earl's house.

"Undoubtedly! But what nonsense! What do you care?" Geoffrey scoffed and then started to laugh. "Although it is an unexpected thrill to see you so devastated, Warrick. For that, I shall never be able to repay you as you've made years of planning and all my pains worth it."

No matter what wicked part she'd played in his downfall, the guilt he felt at her destruction was paralyzing. "All this? Because years ago, I fancied myself in love with Lacey?"

"Was that her name?" the earl asked.

Phillip's gaze narrowed, his rage returning in full force, choking him. Only the footmen's hold kept him from hurling himself at Trent.

"I'd forgotten," Lord Trent admitted softly. "Throw him out and see that he is never admitted to my property again. Good bye, Warrick."

"This isn't the end!" Phillip struggled as the footmen began to haul him backward. "I'll make you pay!"

"Stupid to threaten a man of rank and with witnesses, sir. You'll do no such thing. Or I'll start asking what happened to my sweet little ward and you'll swing from a hangman's noose." Trent's brow furrowed with impatience. "It's ended so prettily, don't spoil my evening, boy! Out!"

They had him through the foyer and pushed down the steps with the added indignity of a beating to ensure that it was all he could do to crawl back onto his horse. The heavens reopened with an icy downpour and before Phillip reached the gate, his stallion was lame.

He dismounted and limped toward the village.

Broken.

A man broken with nothing.

Phillip Warrick was lost.

London 1873

Chapter One

"Please." The man's voice cracked, the tip of his tongue nervously touching his lips as he laid his losing hand of cards on the table and accepted defeat.

Lady Serena Wellcott calmly laid her own cards down. The soft *whick* of the stiff paper meeting the table's firm surface made her smile along with the sight of her quarry flinching in abject misery. "It was not your night. I believe this ends the game, sir."

He shifted in his chair, trying to resummon his dignity. "I'll write you an IOU and see that—"

"No." She shook her head slowly. "That will not satisfy. Not this time."

"The rules of polite society dictate that a gentleman's IOU is always—"

She pulled out her black and emerald beaded reticule and retrieved a dozen small pieces of paper writs in his own handwriting and spread them out in front of her. Serena watched his show of bravado falter and fade at the staggering debt at her fingertips. "It's a heart-stopping sum, is it not, Mr. Hill?"

"You...have all my markers?"

"And I'm calling you on them. Now."

"Oh, god. I'm ruined," he whispered.

"It seems so." She sat back in her chair, primly organizing her paperwork. "But I'm prepared to offer you a solution to your woes, Mr. Hill."

"A solution?" His head came up quickly; his eyes gleaming in the lamplight, anxious for any miraculous solution that would make his financial problems go away.

She almost felt sorry for him.

*Almost.*

"The house in Bath, all its contents and furnishings, the stables and livestock, surrounding land and rents attached to the property. Sign it all over and I'll tear up your markers and consider your debts erased." Serena took a deep breath and simply waited for him to absorb what she'd said.

"B-Bath?" His jaw dropped open in shock. "Impossible! That estate has been in my family for generations."

The tendril of sympathy she'd felt for him died instantly. "Liar. It's been in your *wife's* family for generations."

He stiffened, his face going red. "The house is off the table. I've leveraged it to the hilt and—"

She waved a hand in dismissal. "I'll deal with the creditors once you've done as I ask."

"No! I'll pay you what I can and then—"

She interrupted him again, this time by sweeping the pile of markers back into her purse. "You've mistaken this for a negotiation, Mr. Hill." She lifted a silver bell from the table and rang it.

The door to the private gaming room opened behind her and two identical broad-shouldered muscled hulks wearing matching black suits and coats entered to stand behind their mistress. The door was closed and locked before they transformed into cold sentinels awaiting her next command.

"W-what is the meaning of this?" Mr. Hill demanded, his voice shaking.

"You cannot be that slow of wit, sir," Serena protested, her tone mocking him. "You'll write out the terms I've dictated and your intent to give me all that I've asked and you'll sign it here. Then you'll be at your solicitor's door before the man's had breakfast to make it perfectly legal and binding, delivering the deed into my hands before dinner."

Hill's eyes widened but he said nothing.

"Naturally, Jasper and Jack will be with you at all times for the process to guarantee a successful and flawless transfer of the assets. All of this is to be a confidential transaction in which you will never mention my name or repeat the story of this evening's events to anyone for as long as you draw breath."

The red color drained from his face but to his credit, Mr. Hill salvaged some of his wits. "And if I refuse to play along?"

The twins smiled in perfect unison behind her in a mirthless promise of pain and Serena sighed. "Then they'll kill you. I've never given either of them limitations as to the methods they prefer and for that, the men have assured me that I am their favorite client."

She gave Mr. Hill a chilling smile that underlined her words. "In truth, the boys enjoy their work, sir, so I leave the messy details to them. But no worries. I have requested that in your case, if the worst should come to pass, that they deliver your head in a hatbox to your family so that they'll know to mourn your passing and to tidy up legal matters. You see? I am not completely heartless."

It was all a blatant lie. The twins were muscled props and consummate actors who knew their brutish roles by heart. They hadn't murdered so much as a spider in all the years she'd known them but it didn't matter. She'd yet to meet a man who'd been willing to test their gory claims.

"You bloody bitch! You—" He was on his feet but held in place by the presence of the dangerous brutes at her back. "I'll be ruined! M-my wife...would never forgive me. Sh-she loves that house..."

"If your wife's feelings were truly a priority, perhaps you'd not have leveraged the house and gambled against it in the first place," Serena pointed out, the last of her patience draining away as she also stood from the table. "We have an agreement, Mr. Hill. The house and property in Bath delivered to me before I sit down to dinner."

She calmly adjusted her bonnet to lower the black lace veil over her features and to collect what notes and money remained on the table into her purse.

Hill's fury outweighed his intellect. "Fuck you, you icy whore!"

"Mr. Hill!" Serena gasped, conveying every inch the prim and proper Victorian lady. "Such vile language betrays your true nature!" She readjusted her black kid gloves. "*I've* done nothing to encourage your ruin. I was merely in a position to witness it. Now," she held up her hand and with a slight wave signaled the twins to flank a sputtering and terrified Basil Hill, "I'm assisting you by providing an avenue for you to clear aside this Season's debts quietly and honorably."

"*Honorably?* By calling every marker I had and threatening my life if I don't comply?"

"What threat?  Death is inevitable, sir.  Your life was already fairly worthless from where I'm standing.  You're a weak-willed excuse of a man, grinding away all that Providence had given you and gaily making a party of your failures."  She moved toward him, her voice dropping to a sensual growl.  "Go ahead, Mr. Hill.  Default on our deal.  Do this world the favor and remove yourself from the skin of this earth and shuttle off to the card game in Hell that awaits you.  And don't worry.  I sent the Devil a note with my regards and he's more than happy to save you a seat at his table."

She leaned forward ever so slowly only to spit in his face; abruptly stepping back so that the twins could restrain him from striking out at her.

"By dinner, gentlemen," she said over her shoulder, exiting with an elegant turn of her bustled skirts and sailing out of the room to the sound of Mr. Hill breaking down into braying sobs while her henchmen silently stood by.

She stepped from the exclusive gambling house into the damp night air and then down the steps to her waiting carriage without breaking her stride.  The ride through London's streets gave her time to close her eyes and replay the scene with Hill until she was confident that no detail had been omitted.

By the time she arrived at her sumptuous London home, the fleeting rush of triumph had quieted to remind her that until the title to the Bath property was in hand, she should remain alert and prepared for anything.

"Good evening, your ladyship," her butler greeted her as he took her fur trimmed cloak and hat. "Are you in for the evening, madam?"

"I am in, Mr. Quinn. I'll have a note to go out and then lock the house." Serena retreated up the stairs as the clocks in the house struck three in the morning, not sparing a single glance to the luxury around her. Her steps were quiet on the carpeted floors and by the time she reached the sanctuary of her rooms on the first floor, Serena felt the first pangs of exhaustion.

It had been a good night's work but it had come after weeks of intense planning.

"You look done in," Pepper commented as she met her inside the bedroom doorway. "Shall I run a bath to help you sleep?"

"I'll forgo it."

"And forgo any rest, I'll warrant," Pepper groused softly.

"I don't need a nanny! I'll sleep like the dead, now stop fussing." Serena's imperious tone was meaningless to her ladies maid. For seven years, Miss Pepper Collins had been her closest companion and sole confidant. She had no closer ally in the world than the little country beauty and Serena was grateful for her care.

Serena crossed to her desk and sat down to draft one quick message.

*"It is accomplished."*

The note was sealed with a dollop of black wax and Serena pressed the brass circle with an engraved rose into the soft surface to make the mark of the Black Rose Society.

"Here, take this to Quinn and tell him to make sure that it cannot be traced back to this house." She held up the sealed note for Pepper to take downstairs. "And then come back up and draw my bath."

Pepper smiled sweetly at the rare victory and curtsied before leaving to tend to her errand.

"It is accomplished," she repeated to the empty room, attempting to recall the fleeting joy she'd felt when Hills had wept.

But joy eluded her.

Mrs. Hill's family holdings and lands were now secured from her wastrel of a husband's grasp. No drunken impulse or lure of the cards would ever again threaten her future or that of her two daughters.

And the Black Rose would have a new member in Mrs. Hill and access to a lovely home in Bath or to any of the resources Mrs. Hill held on their behalf. It was the price of her services that any recipient would yield without question or hesitation to any future requests she made or from anyone bearing her signet ring.

Lady Serena Wellcott had founded the Black Rose Reading Society five years before with a clear understanding that a literary club would be overlooked by most of her peers and would provide a benign excuse for women to gather without scrutiny. For the Black Rose had nothing to do with literature and the discussion of books—and everything to do with revenge.

And power.

In the world as she knew it, women held almost no power. Legally one step above livestock, they held almost no sway beyond the domestic sphere and even there, Serena believed that their control over their own fates was an illusion.

A woman's intellect, wit, and sexuality were the obvious tools of the game. Pepper returned and within moments had divested Serena of the layers of expensive silk and confining undergarments that she wore like armor. It was impossible not to sigh at the sweet relief of being able to take a deep breath unencumbered and to slide into her silk wrap.

"Did he cry?" the maid asked.

She nodded, smiling. "Like a toddler."

"Brilliant," Pepper sighed.

"You are an easy woman to please, Miss Prudence. You realize this?" Serena teased as she retied her dressing gown. "But then, aren't we all?"

Pepper's nose wrinkled at the use of her proper Christian name. "I'll get your bath drawn. Wait here and try not to work." Pepper left her at the vanity to brush her hair out and Serena disregarded the jibe.

*Vengeance is an unforgiving mistress—and cares nothing for the clock.*

Even so, she didn't want to give Pepper the satisfaction of demonstrating her inability to avoid the pile of petitions and letters calling to her from her desk, so she deliberately picked up the brush and tended to her curls.

Something in her reflection stopped her hand mid-stroke and Serena leaned closer to study the woman peering back at her in the glass.

*There.*

*There's that wicked creature.*

She smiled and the beauty in the mirror smiled unabashedly back. Her hair fell in long black curls that a gypsy would have envied and framed aristocratic features spoiled by pale blue eyes that appeared almost silver-grey. Lush porcelain lines and firm curves highlighted the powers of a woman in her prime at a mere twenty-four years of age and she well knew the nuances of every flutter of an eyelash or tilt of a chin to wield those powers to her advantage.

She deliberately slid back the silk of one sleeve to bare one shoulder and her breath caught in her throat.

*There.*

For she didn't see Lady Serena Wellcott, an independent woman of wealth enjoying her life amidst the glittering world of the Ton and London's elite while she pursued only the most proper entertainments and dabbled in a social cause here and there when it suited her.

She saw Raven Wells, bastard born and as wild as the fens. A child that had known nothing but betrayal and the twists of cruel games until she'd learned the truth of it at seventeen years of age to become the mistress of her own games.

Revenge wasn't something a woman pursued on a lark or in a fleeting snit.

Raven had been taught by the best what it meant to be used and abandoned, her emotions regarded as meaningless and her worth measured only by how clever a pawn she could be.

"All ready for you," Pepper's announcement interrupted her thoughts.

"Yes. I'm ready, too."

Chapter Two

Serena made another, more thorough study of the young woman

sitting across from her. In the guise of a social call, Mrs. Delilah

Osborne sat nervously gathering her wits to make her case.

"Go on." Lady Wellcott signaled Pepper to leave the teacart

and began to serve them both from the painted porcelain set

without bothering to ask the woman's preferences. Serena had sat

through enough of these meetings to know that Mrs. Osborne

would graciously accept whatever was handed to her and then

forget to take a single sip.

"Mrs. Standish referred me…I meant to say, there was a

conversation about how d-difficult it was to keep a good maid in

service these days and…" Mrs. Osborne cleared her throat, a

miserable picture in her modestly sturdy visiting dress and

tastefully unattractive bonnet. "She was a longtime friend of my

mother's or I would never have accidentally confided in her. But she was very firm in her advice and insisted that I should call on you. She said that you would have a ready solution."

Serena held out the obligatory cup of tea with milk and sugar and smiled as the young woman took it without question. "Mrs. Standish is very clever and well-informed. But I cannot speak of the possibility of solutions until I know the problem." She collected her own cup with the grace of a geisha. "Pretend that *I* am a longtime friend, Mrs. Osborne, and confide in me."

"Of course," she nodded her head, her cheeks flushing a flattering shade of pink. "It's just such a sordid horrible business…"

Serena smiled. "Naturally. If it were a simple matter, then a good woman such as yourself would see to it directly and have no need of someone like me."

"Someone like you," her guest echoed softly, a wariness coming into her countenance.

*Good. She's paying attention.*

"Tell me what you're thinking, Mrs. Osborne."

"I'm thinking that I am in over my head and quite without options. This all seems a bit strange but as I look at you, I wonder if Mrs. Standish hasn't made a mistake. You are so much younger than I expected. You seem very kind but I don't see how there is anything you can do to help me with...the situation. And," she let out an unsteady sigh as she set down her untouched tea. "I've abused the time allotted for a social call and should be making an awkward exit instead of sitting here stammering on your sofa."

"Nonsense!" Serena set down her own cup hard enough to rattle the china against the marble surface of the cart. "I hate the rules about allotted times and a person's ability to come and go as they please! Five minutes is hardly time to get your skirts arranged and begin any proper conversation and then off people go in a tangle of wraps and bonnets spitting out niceties and meaningless platitudes about hospitality. A waste of an afternoon, if you ask me!"

"Oh!" Mrs. Osborne's surprise was charming.

"But you didn't come here to waste my time or your own, Mrs. Osborne. Did you? Mrs. Standish said nothing beyond a note with your name to confirm that she spoke to you. But you've come because you have a dreadful problem that," Serena paused only long enough to re-evaluate her guest and apply her uncanny talent for observation, "by the look of it is robbing you of sleep and your health. And if it's to do with your current lady's maid, then I already have my suspicions. For you are impeccably put together so her skills aren't in question, even if I must urge you to choose richer colors for I swear those pastels make you look positively ill, Mrs. Osborne."

Mrs. Osborne blushed. "I…like pastels."

"They do not return your affections," she said smiling and was finally rewarded with a shy smile in return as the young Mrs. Osborne caught on to her hostess's keen wit and sense of humor. "Is it your current lady's maid that is involved?"

Mrs. Osborne nodded, her eyes filling with tears.

Serena sighed. "And your husband."

It wasn't a question. She just had to understand the boundaries of the issue. Her instincts were screaming but the truth had to be spoken aloud by Mrs. Osborne.

*Her husband's at her maid and probably other girls in the house. If it were a mutual affair or sinful dalliance, she wouldn't have that sick look in her eyes and she'd have already sent the girl packing.*

"He…" Mrs. Osborne took a deep breath and let it all out as the tears slipped down her cheeks. "I know it is not an uncommon abuse of power for…men to…approach young women in service and I am not blind to it. I…confronted him the first year we were married when I learned that he'd…taken advantage of one of the younger kitchen maids."

"And what did he say?"

"That it was none of my concern. That I should mind my tone and not make myself appear stupid by taking the word of an uneducated child over his when it came to such, as he put it, 'ridiculous accusations'." Mrs. Osborne's hands were clenched into fists in her lap so tightly that Serena could see the threads in the seams of her gloves from the strain. "And I…complied and then convinced myself that it was a singular occurrence."

"But it wasn't." Serena encouraged her to continue.

Mrs. Osborne shook her head, shame choking her answer into a single word. "No."

"How many "singular occurrences" have there been?" Serena leaned forward a single inch, her gaze locked onto the misery in her guest's face.

"Many I think, but…the last. He raped my dear Dell. She—she has been with me as my personal maid since I was fifteen and when I found her…crying on the floor in my dressing room…I couldn't stay silent any longer. God forgive me for all the others, but Dell, she is more than a maid. She's been like a sister to me."

"Why not dismiss her? For her own safety?"

"I can't! I wanted to—though it would break my heart—I'd have seen her to another situation and guaranteed her placement with a glowing letter of recommendation but…"

"She's pregnant and there's not a respectable house in London that will hire a lady's maid in her current state." Serena finished for her, sparing Mrs. Osborne the agony of it.

Mrs. Osborne nodded. "My sweet Dell! I cannot turn her out now! But if he learns of her condition, he won't be as merciful! I know him too well."

Serena held out a lace edged handkerchief and Mrs. Osborne took it gratefully.

"Thank you."

Serena sighed. "I'm going to pace about, Mrs. Osborne. I say it in advance only because I've had more than one guest misinterpret my standing to some kind of dismissal when that's not my intention at all." She stood and smoothed out her skirts. "It helps me think to move about."

Mrs. Osborne nodded, dabbing her eyes with the soft linen square. "Then please do."

Serena smiled and walked to the window, absorbing how much she liked Mrs. Delilah Osborne. It wasn't a requirement to like a petitioner but it never hurt. The urgency of the situation pressed against her heart and Serena had to take a few deep breaths to keep her emotions clear of the tangle. Even so, there was one question she had to ask to make sure there were on the same page.

"You're not asking me for a referral to a cooperative physician, are you? You're not seeking to end this child?" she asked, as neutral as stone.

"No!" Mrs. Osborne shifted in her chair, nearly coming to her feet in indignation at the question but holding her place all the same. "I-I know it's done but—Dell couldn't face such a thing and I...I have no children of my own, Lady Wellcott. Years of hoping for a baby have made them seem far more precious to me, even in these horrifying circumstances, I refuse to see a life squandered."

"Very well." Serena began her pacing in earnest. As a bastard herself, she had an affinity for innocent children robbed of a name and had planned on pressing Mrs. Osborne into providing for the child or even allowing Serena to make arrangements for its care. "We'll set aside the topic of the babe for the time being."

"Dell is a very good girl, Lady Wellcott."

"Of course, she is." Serena crossed the room, listening to the rustling of her skirts and savoring this part of the game. Problems were one thing but the crafting of a wicked solution was nothing short of thrilling. "Is she safe from him now?"

"I believe so. I'm keeping her close, even when I go out shopping or on errands but there's no telling really. James is usually more interested in conquest than he is in affairs." Mrs. Osborne's hands tightened in her lap again. "I've done my best to distract him."

Serena turned, eyeing Mrs. Osborne with new respect. "Dell is lucky to have you."

"Can you help her?  Could you…perhaps take her on yourself until the child is born or—"

"I do not believe in temporary solutions, Mrs. Osborne," Serena interrupted her.

Mrs. Osborne's disappointment was as apparent as a cloud covering the sun.  "Oh."

"Your maid is not the only woman in trouble, madam." Serena went over to the sideboard and poured two glasses of wine. "The problem is your husband.  He must be stopped and quickly to prevent Dell's ejection from your home and to protect the other women in your service, as well as yourself.  Do you love him?"

The question was a bit abrupt but it was meant to be, evoking an honest reaction from Mrs. Osborne.

"No!  What?  J-James?  I…couldn't…I should not say, Lady Wellcott."

"Then no, you don't," Serena said with a smile and brought Mrs. Osborne one of the crystal goblets.  "You'd have looked miserable and confessed it rather than sitting there and looking shocked and horrified at the very notion."

"Why do you ask such things?" She took the glass, this time taking a small sip for courage.

"Because if you engage my services, Mrs. Osborne, then I must know exactly what the boundaries are and how far you will be willing to go to achieve our goal."

"And what is the goal?" Mrs. Osborne asked, a woman mystified and enthralled.

"Justice." Serena took a sip of her wine and sat back down. "Now, *this*, Mrs. Osborne is the moment where I shall tell you that you are free to take your leave if you disagree. This is the moment where you can profess to have misunderstood my intentions and withdraw without judgment. Naturally, I'd advise you to *never* repeat a word of our conversation since I would simply deny it and act defensively and without qualms to ensure that you withdrew the tale." She crossed her ankles very daintily. "But if you agree that justice is in fact the path we must take to see that these vicious attacks never occur again under your roof against the women who have entrusted themselves to your care…"

Mrs. Osborne nodded slowly. "He must be stopped."

"I *can* and will stop him, madam. But let me be clear. I am a merciless thing and before I'm done, your James will wish that he had never been born. This is not a polite game of subtle pressure and silly strategies. I want him to suffer for what he's done to your Dell and to all the women before her. Only the darkest flavor of vengeance will satisfy my appetite after hearing your tale and while a woman with a softer nature might flinch—I have no qualms about plotting a man's destruction. There is no act or sin off the table or beyond consideration if it brings me closer to achieving what I want. None. Do you understand me, Mrs. Osborne?"

Delilah Osborne was solemn and still. "You'll destroy him."

It wasn't a question but a quest for affirmation.

"I will."

Mrs. Osborne took a larger swallow from her glass before setting it on the cart. "And what is the going rate for justice, Lady Wellcott?"

"Mostly, its greatest cost is your pledge to keep our arrangements strictly secret. But once we have done as promised, then you will be a member in the Black Rose Reading Society and will vow to help any other member who approaches you with a need and to provide *whatever* they ask without question." Serena quickly tossed back the contents of her own glass before setting it down next to Mrs. Osborne's. "The Black Rose is a small women's circle dedicated to helping one another with life's more vexing problems. Where the law of the land turns a blind eye to the plight of women, the Black Rose Reading Society stands quietly ready to hear any petition and tries to act where we can."

"The Black Rose Reading Society. It all sounds so tidy," Mrs. Osborne said quietly.

"From one perspective, it is," Serena conceded. "But from another…"

"Consider yourself employed, Lady Wellcott."

Serena smiled. "Good." She held out her hand to Mrs. Osborne. "We shall shake on it and call it a contract."

Mrs. Osborne took her hand shyly. "Just that? I'm not to…sign anything?" she asked.

Serena shook her head. "There shall be no written trace of our agreement. Well, perhaps one small thing."

"And what is that?"

"Are you still in London this late in the season or has your husband retreated to the country?" Serena asked.

"We leave London tomorrow. Is that—a problem?" Delilah replied with a new flush of color in her cheeks.

"Not at all. You must send me an invitation to visit your country estates, Mrs. Osborne. Tell your husband you have made a new friend in London and that I expressed an interest in your gardens."

"Of course," Mrs. Osborne said. "James will be quite impressed that I've managed a friendship with a lady of your station. He's always accused me of lacking social ambition."

"Perfect." Serena stood, this time effectively ending the visit. "I'll see you again soon, Mrs. Osborne. I look forward to my country holiday."

"Thank you, Lady Wellcott. Thank you for—"

"Don't! Don't thank me until I've honored my promises."

"As you wish." Mrs. Osborne curtsied and left. "Good day, Lady Wellcott."

Serena sat for a few moments alone sifting through the implications of her new commitment and her own plans averted until Pepper cleared her throat from the open doorway. "Yes, Pepper. Let's have it."

"Lucky chance, that."

"Lucky?" She smiled and shook her head slowly in subtle denial. "How am I lucky today?"

"I struck a good conversation with your visitor's driver and learned a great deal. It seems Mrs. Osborne was a Fitzpatrick before her wedding."

A strange icy tendril unfurled down Serena's spine. "Make it plain."

"She is cousin to a Sir Phillip Warrick, your ladyship."

The world stopped and Serena stood in a rush, all the color draining from her cheeks. "You're certain?"

Pepper nodded. "As certain as I am of my own toes."

"Hellfire," Serena's fingers moved to touch the racing pulse at her throat. "There's a twist."

"Do you—wish me to stay?"

"No. I need a moment alone." She turned away before the maid answered, confident of the woman's loyalty and obedience. Her mind was racing as the past rushed in and robbed her of all her icy reserve.

*Damn.*

*Phillip Warrick. Just your name and I am there again.*

*In love.*

*In loathing.*

*God help me, it's all there and all proof that I wasn't an idiot for putting this off.*

For years, she'd done nothing but craft revenge for others, while quietly feeding her own need for justice. With every cruel twist, she'd imagined that it was her own satisfaction she'd achieved. But that fleeting joy never lasted.

The only sound in the room was the tick of the clock over the mantelpiece and the drumming of her own heartbeat in her ears. She'd always prided herself on her planning and her control of every element in the new life she'd crafted, but luck had wrested away the illusion once and for all. Pepper was correct in crowing over the simple twist. Chance had brought things back around and if luck held, the world would right itself again.

*Not that I won't neglect to lend it a hand.*

Serena deliberately took a few deep breaths and waited until the feeling finally uncurled inside of her.

*There.*

*There it is. That first little hint of the thrill of the hunt.*

*And the promise of joy.*

Chapter Three

"Purgatory probably has better landscaping," Phillip Warrick

growled as he reined in his horse to stop some distance from his

cousin's house. He readjusted his hat and pressed one gloved hand

against his eyes to fight off his fatigue.

He hated the press of family obligations almost as much as

he hated most of his family, but his great aunt was one of the few

adorable exceptions and he held her esteem too dear to risk

offense. Great Aunt Bella had written him a letter laced with

gentle pleas that he make an effort underlined with nothing short of

the steel of a general's marching orders.

*"Go to your cousin's for a visit. If I hear you've retreated*

*to your Lake Country house without stopping, I shall demand your*

*reasons in person, dear nephew. I am too old to make threats but*

*be assured that I will cry nightly until I hear that my favorite boy*

*has graced my grandson's door."*

"Tears," he sighed. "God, why is it that at any age from nine to ninety, women always resort to tears." His horse's ears pricked back and the stallion neighed as if to reply, making Phillip laugh.

"Yes, I know! Because it always works!" He spurred his mount to bring about a quick end to the journey. Truthfully, it wasn't his relatives in particular he hated. It was the prying into his life and the endless pressure for him to "amend his ways" and marry as he should. The family had clung to the edges of the peerage for so long that ambition had become second nature for most of the Warricks. Since he'd been in long pants it had been made clear to him that his future required him to achieve some proper rich cow to uphold the family honor and fortify their status. He was the head of the family, or the head of the mess as he liked to call it and Phillip was expected to do his part to pull them up or at the very least, see to it that they didn't slip any further down the social ladder.

When he was younger, it had felt like a grand game. He'd even had romantic notions of finding a true love that would make everyone happy, most especially himself. But when that proved disastrous, he'd abandoned hope and given in to a life that largely omitted social tangles and instead focused entirely on managing his holdings.

Except when it made Aunt Bella cry.

The house came into view and Phillip drew up to an impromptu welcome as James Osborne came down the grand stone steps to greet him. "Cousin! Your arrival is nearly unprecedented in its anticipation since Homer wrote of the 'Odyssey'! My god, the women of the house are driving me mad with their speculation about your appearance!"

Phillip grit his teeth but did his best to smile. "Then I'm sure to disappoint. Odysseus is mortal with mud on his boots and if you think for one moment I'm slaying anything more threatening than a good glass of brandy, you've lost your wits."

James' laughter rang out and he clapped Phillip's shoulder as if they were long lost companions. "There's that wicked humor I remember. How long has it been?"

"Two years since I was tricked into spending Christmas here because your grandmother made it sound like Cousin Delilah was dying. If I recall it right, she had a cold."

"Ah, your dear Grandmother! She does have a way with words!" James waved off the deception. "Well, you'll be glad you're here this time! It turns out that for once, my social connections may be improving—without your help, you cold-hearted bastard! We've another guest who's arrived just a few days ago. My dull little wife has somehow lured out a titled young lady who is filthy rich by all accounts!" James smiled. "Perhaps you can apply some of that infamous charisma of yours and see about sweeping her off her feet!"

Phillip gave him a quelling look, not only for his ham-fisted foray into matchmaking, but for the unkind remark about Delilah. He'd always liked his pretty cousin's quiet ways and where everyone else made free with their scathing comments and judgments, Delilah simply made him welcome and ensured he had his favorite biscuits at tea time. "Where is the delightful Delilah? I must thank her for her correspondence and for the birthday gift. She was the only one to recall the day, did you know that?"

James stiffened at the reprimand. "I believe she is in the music room with Lady Wellcott. As I said, Lady Wellcott is very—"

"Enough of that! Lead on." Phillip squared his shoulders. He'd meet the woman and be civil but he was not about to skip and dance at James' direction.

Southgate was a fine home if not the most impressive by the county's standards. Phillip liked its layout and if he hadn't made it a habit to keep his distance, he might have come more often for its comforts. James led him into the ivory room on the ground floor with its cheery view of the gardens

"Look who I found, Delilah! Cousin Phillip is here and now the sighs can cease!" James spread his arms like a magician presenting a rabbit from his pockets.

Delilah left her chair by the windows to rush toward him for the warmest of hugs. "Dear cousin, I am so glad to see you again!"

"You grow lovelier each time." He kissed her cheek and then froze as a figure in the corner of his vision also rose from her seat. It was a ghost who had mercilessly haunted his dreams but who had never before manifested so brazenly in his waking hours.

Delilah mistook the shift in his attention and stepped back with a smile. "May I introduce you to my friend, Lady Serena Wellcott? Lady Wellcott, this is my cousin, Sir Phillip Warrick."

"Sir Warrick." She gracefully held out her hand and he walked forward to take it, bowing stiffly over to brush his lips across flesh that he'd mourned as dead by a lonely roadside seven years ago.

He nodded, his voice gone. It was surreal. Raven Wells was within reach, lovelier and more sensually potent than any woman had a right to be. The intervening years had heightened her powers, all of the soft edges of youth melting into a woman of incomparable beauty. Her ebony black hair was twisted up into a delicate crown of braids without a single curl out of place. The aristocratic features he had so admired were turned toward him, her serene countenance daring him to take note of porcelain skin without the insult of powders and lips the wickedest color of red coral. And her eyes...

*God, those eyes! How did I ever think to forget those icy gray eyes?*

It was clear that despite all his horrified conclusions of her fate after months of fruitless searching years ago; the lady had obviously flourished and landed on her feet.

*Like a cat.*

She laughed at something Delilah said and Phillip struggled to unclench his hands at his sides. The melody of her laughter threatened to unman him. He wanted to seize her shoulders and shake her, to punish her, to possess her, to demand an explanation, beg her for forgiveness and to hear her pleas for mercy and cries in regret at her betrayal. He wanted all those things at once and none of it was possible.

"Phillip?" Delilah asked, a gentle touch on his arm relaying her concern. "Is everything all right?"

One breath. His life turned on the edge of this moment. If he called her out, it would be like pulling a loose thread on a tapestry he could never repair. Confronting her was a fleeting option as she stood there, dressed like a duchess holding court while his dear cousin sat meekly at her side. It was clear that Delilah and her husband were enamored of the 'grand lady' in their midst, and it was all he could do not to shout his fury at the deception.

But there was more to it than that.

Because one look at him with those bewitching silvery eyes and it was as if time held still. Every desire he'd ever felt for her multiplied at the denial of years, the cruel loss she'd inflicted on him and the staggering guilt he still harbored at her destruction.

*There's a tiger in the music room and they think she's a housecat.*

"Everything is fine." He forced himself to smile. "I'm just a bit mortified to meet your guest while I still have the mud of the road on my coat. James was so eager…"

"Think nothing of it," Lady Wellcott said. "Mud is nothing if not humbling and I've yet to meet a man who doesn't improve with its touch."

His jaw tightened. "I do strive to improve."

Her smile sent a wicked shiver of hunger and anger down his spine. "Don't lose heart, Sir Warrick. Admitting that you fall short is half of the battle, is it not?"

"Phillip does not fall short by any means." Delilah came to his defense. "He is all that is noble and worthy in my eyes."

"Is he indeed?" Lady Wellcott said, her eyebrows lifting in surprise.

"I am sure you will become good friends," Delilah said. "Phillip is very dear to me."

"Of course he is," James said, openly displeased. "God, are we really going to stand about and discuss how wonderful your cousin is? This is tedious conversation for a man to bear, ladies."

"I'm happy to leave off," Phillip said quickly then took a step back. "If you'll excuse me, I'll see about changing my clothes. Improvement or no, these splashes of humility on my boots are not adding to the beauty of your music room." He bowed slightly and risked one last look at Lady Serena Wellcott. "I so look forward to further conversation, your ladyship."

*And to wiping that arrogant smile off of your face, Raven Wells.*

She nodded her head, a phantom of a salute to demonstrate her good breeding. "Sir Warrick. A pleasure to meet you."

Innocuous words but at the sound of the word 'pleasure' on her ripe lips, Phillip's stomach spasmed with heat. *Damn it! This is ridiculous!*

He couldn't answer her, so he turned and left without another word, cursing the sensation that he was trapped in a social nightmare. Phillip had never told anyone in his family of his affair with Raven Wells. The witnesses at the party had all naturally assumed that there had been some falling out between the pair when their departure from Oakwell Manor had not been followed by a marriage announcement. The few questions he'd faced had been easy to deter and Phillip cringed now recalling how he had lied and said that the lady had changed her mind and broken the engagement.

The story guaranteed him the listener's sympathy but also an end to the conversation since no one wanted to push a man on such a painful subject. No one had ever pressed him on what might have become of the lady and Phillip endured the silence, hiding his heartache.

And now as she manifested in his cousin's house, he saw what a mistake it was to have harbored that secret. Raven Wells had used the time to reinvent herself and perfect her craft. There were hardly any traces of the impulsive smiling girl he'd kissed in a gazebo and pursued with a singular madness.

*Working some scheme, pretending to be something she is not and setting everyone around her up like pins in a bowling game.*

Chapter Four

"How are you faring, Mrs. Osborne?" Serena said as she set her

parasol on her shoulder to shield any view of their conversation

from the house. The women had set out on a stroll in Southgate's

gardens and it was the perfect setting for a private exchange.

"I wish I could say," Delilah replied. "I was so terrified

that James would question your visit or suspect something. But it

has gone so well, so why then do I feel no relief? Only more

concern that I've pulled another woman into this mess?"

"It is only natural to experience anxiety." Serena allowed a

few moments to pass, the rhythmic crunch of the gravel path a

strange music underneath it all. "But I am settled in and welcomed

by your husband without a ripple of resistance."

"No ripple except for Cousin Phillip." Delilah smiled. "I

never expected him to accept my invitation and apparently he

thinks this all some grand matchmaking scheme. I apologize, Lady

Wellcott. My family has hounded him for years on the matter and he is surly when he is cornered."

"Ah! Poor man," Serena said as warmly as she could. "It is a relief to think I have not given offense to Sir Warrick."

"Oh, no! I cannot imagine such a thing! I'm sure it is only his stubborn attachment to bachelorhood that inspired his social lapse at your introduction. But I can assure you that Phillip is the kindest of men and a true gentleman."

Serena was forced to pretend to be diverted by a nearby rose bush. "Of course. In any case, we shall be happy for the distraction when it comes to your husband. With male company to divert him, I have more latitude to act."

"Do you have a plan then?"

"Not yet." Serena bent over to smell a crimson rose the color of blood, inhaling the power of its fragrance. "But I have several ideas."

"Thank God!"

Serena straightened to give her friend a saucy look. "I can assure you, Mrs. Osborne that God will be the last one I would consult for this enterprise. Though if I have my way, your husband will send up a few prayers for His mercy by the time we're done."

"Oh! You do say the most shocking things, Lady Wellcott!"

"If I have already shocked you, then I fear what your reaction will be to my next suggestion."

"Please. Speak without fear."

"Mrs. Osborne, I need you to become unavailable to your husband. Starting today, he must find no relief in your bed and no avenue for his desires." Serena waited as her blunt request struck home.

Delilah nodded assent, a blush creeping up her throat to touch her cheeks. "James is—it is not easy to dissuade him, madam. His appetite for…marital relations is…quite vigorous."

"Good. Then its withdrawal will make it easier to work against him." Serena smiled and motioned for them to continue walking. "Tell him you have your monthly flow or better yet, confess that you harbor some nebulous hope that you are carrying his child which makes you fearful of the exercise. From what I've observed, he still has great ambitions that a son of his will overtake

Sir Warrick as head of your family one day. Especially if Sir Warrick remains unmarried, am I right?"

"It is true," Delilah whispered. "Though I suspect he is equally anxious that Cousin Phillip marry well and fill the family's coffers. It is a dilemma of conscience for James."

"Then we have him on both fronts. He may protest being banished from your bed but he won't cross it. And if his libido is as strong as you say, then it's a matter of days before his desires will make him ripe for the picking."

"As easy as that?"

Serena shook her head. "It does seem a bit too simple. But it never hurts to have a man's own blood working against his nerves before you move against him."

"Are you going to seduce him, Lady Wellcott?" Delilah asked in horrified astonishment.

Serena shrugged her shoulders. "Perhaps. But only to scratch his face for it and scream for the magistrate, Mrs. Osborne."

"Oh, that would be—brilliant!" Delilah sighed. "But the scandal! Would you not be publicly ruined in the course of it?"

"That is for me to manage, Mrs. Osborne."

"I am so grateful." Delilah's eyes brimmed with unshed tears. "If I had the strength to act alone…"

"You are very strong, Delilah. Do not doubt your courage—or your wisdom. Guard what light and grace you can in your soul for it is precious and irreplaceable. There is no shame in summoning someone who can shield you from the worst and withstand the blows. I have no light left to mourn its loss, Mrs. Osborne. But I can admire women who possess it and take pride in defending the goodness in them when I can."

"You refer to yourself as if you are a lost cause." Delilah shook her head. "I do not believe that, Lady Wellcott."

"You are too kind," she said and the gravel's song beneath her feet grounded out a noise that to her ears sounded like, *"Too kind, too bad, too kind, too bad."*

*Let us hope that Mrs. Osborne does not lose that belief before this is all over.*

"I should get back to the house," Delilah said. "I'm to go over the menus with the cook and I wanted to ensure that Dell is holding up under the strain."

"By all means. I am enjoying the exercise and will see you tonight at dinner."

Delilah kissed her on the cheek and left her at the entrance to a long vine covered walkway. Serena watched her go until she was out of sight and closed her parasol to enter the shaded archway.

Privacy was a thing to savor. Serena forced herself to ignore the maelstrom that was her past and instead concentrate on the challenge of bringing James Osborne to heel. If his perverted inclination was to prefer taking a woman by force, then openly flirting with the bastard would probably be counterproductive. Perhaps a suggestion of—

"If you're up to something, if you intend to harm me by ingratiating yourself to James or Delilah, I'll have you know that—
"

Serena turned at the sound of Phillip's voice, briefly startled before she laughed to cut him off. "My goodness, Sir Warrick! What a ridiculous thing to say!"

"It's not ridiculous! I haven't forgotten what happened, Raven Wells. I haven't forgotten what you…are."

"And what am I?" she asked, her expression calm, her eyes clear.

"You're a grifter and a con-artist! You and Trent would have had me publicly ruined if I hadn't finally seen through the scheme!" It was an old wound but it still stung. She'd hurt far more than his pride and there wasn't a day since when he hadn't thought of her, either to curse her or ache with the memories of young love.

She shook her head slowly and deliberately walked back out into the sun drenched path. "I don't know what surprises me most. That you are still somehow so self-righteous to believe yourself the wounded party in that long ago drama or that you think I'm going to crumble after you sputter and spit insults at me." She opened her parasol with a practiced flick of her wrist and rested it on her shoulder, framing her face and shielding her from the sun.

If it was calculated to enhance her beauty, it had worked but the effect made him feel even angrier. "You'll crumble after they toss you out as an imposter!" he countered.

"An imposter?" Serena looked at him in dramatic shock. "But that's ridiculous, Sir Warrick. I am, *in fact*, Lady Wellcott and I am, in fact, quite wealthy—rich far beyond your family's meager holdings. The name and title are *legally* mine and I can provide countless references to prove all, if you require them. I am exactly as you see and while I hate to disappoint you, I honestly had no idea of your connection to Mrs. Osborne when I accepted her invitation. A rare mistake I won't repeat." She shrugged her shoulders prettily. "As for Trent, I haven't seen him since that time. It seems you have something in common with the earl."

She tipped her head to one side as if studying him and Phillip couldn't help but remember the familiar tip of her chin and the way she'd once studied how best to please him.

"Do I?"

"Yes, more than you know. For you both took what you wanted and never bothered to look back." She took a small dismissive step back. "As for the current awkwardness, by all means, let us go in and tell your cousin of our sordid connection. I am sure they will be riveted to hear of your liaison with a seventeen year old girl without resources or family and of your intended elopement. Engagements are broken so often these days without much scandal, perhaps they won't blink to learn of your skills at seduction and kidnapping."

*Damn.*

"There was—more to it than that."

"Of course. But you don't really want to have that conversation, do you, Phillip?"

He held his ground. "You deliberately deceived me. Lord Trent was your ally and you… You were not who or what you seemed. Don't play it now as if you were innocent in—"

She leapt like a cat closing the distance between them, her eyes sparking with a fury that caught him off guard because part of the shine in her gaze was unshed tears. "I *was* innocent! I was—" She clapped her fingers against her lips to stop her own speech, turning away from him to hide her face. "This exchange is at an end. Make your confessions to your family if you wish. I'm not interested in hearing them."

She walked away and he realized that his mouth was open like a fish.

Chapter Five

Serena returned to the house, ignoring several questioning looks

from the servants on the stairs and in the hall, as she practically

raced to the sanctuary of her chambers. It was a testament to her

monumental self-discipline that she didn't slam the bedroom door

behind her but even in her rage, she knew better.

She'd already made a show of leaving him in the garden

and slamming doors like a spoiled child would only fuel the

servants' gossip. And forfeit any ground she'd gained in their

encounter.

Seven years.

Seven years since she'd seen him or heard his voice or been

within reach of his hands…

She couldn't count how many times she'd played out

potential exchanges or daydreamed about what she would say

when she finally met him again. In most of her fantasies, she'd been in command of the situation or revealed herself after an elaborate trap had been sprung to destroy him. In dark daydreams, with a multitude looking on she had a heeled boot on his neck while he whined of his undying remorse and unworthiness for hurting her…

*Why did I not think of something so mundane as meeting him in a drawing room or walking in a garden? Why did my wits desert me when I needed them most?*

"So he's here? Your Sir Warrick?"

"He's here and he is most decidedly not *my* anything."

"Well, I admit I didn't think he'd pop up so quickly. If he's here then won't that interfere with any plans you have for—"

"It changes nothing. He means nothing. I'd have dealt with him soon enough but for now, my commitment to Mrs. Osborne is unaltered. Let him stew and fret."

"Will he not say something to Mr. Osborne?"

Serena shook her head. "No. He can't without exposing his own transgressions in the affair and…" She slowly opened her jewelry chest, the gleam and glitter of her treasures coming to life in the candlelight. "I am counting on Mr. Osborne's ambitions to keep him in check. Phillip may be the male heir and head of the family but it's his Achilles heel as well. They'll see me as a potential catch and keep a tight hold on the reins if he starts to growl or fuss."

She lifted out a diamond-encrusted choker she usually saved for extremely formal parties. "We shall dress to impress, Pepper, and make sure Sir Warrick understands who holds the whip hand."

The diamonds were a wise choice, Phillip told himself grudgingly. Raven was playing the lady with a flair that denied even a breath of suspicion. James was so enthralled by the glittering show of wealth at his table, the man was practically salivating. He watched her in reluctant appreciation then glanced over at his cousin Delilah who was looking at him in silent supplication to behave better toward her new friend.

*And there's the answer.*

*Oh, I can behave 'better'. In fact, I can play the part that will send James into paroxysms of joy and ensure that whatever schemes the witch is cooking will come to nothing but ashes. You should have run, Raven, while you had the chance.*

"I must say, Lady Wellcott," Phillip interjected at the first pause in the conversation. "Had I known that Aphrodite herself was going to grace this house, I would have brought a better wardrobe."

Serena smiled. "Is it your opinion that the goddess of love would be swayed by a better waistcoat?"

"It may not hurt."

"What shallow flavor of love are you aiming at, Sir Warrick?" she countered, not giving him an inch.

"Then school me, Lady Wellcott. What does sway a woman of substance?" he asked.

"A man out of his waistcoat is always a good start." The look she gave him was so potent with heated challenge that Phillip had to shift in his chair at the surge of stiffening blood rushing to his cock. "And naturally, an invitation to take a grown man to school strikes me as a thing that has an appeal all its own. Would you not agree, Mrs. Osborne?"

"Oh!" Delilah exclaimed. "I—have no opinion on such things."

Lady Wellcott lifted her wine glass to her lips and set it down slowly. "Oh, well. Do not fear. Your cousin makes a show of flirting with me but like most men, he will shy away from any real challenge." She picked up her knife to make an elegant slice across the venison on her plate. "Men easily speak of goddesses and then manage to look so handsome in their surprise when a woman demands to be worshipped. But don't worry, Sir Warrick. I neither expect you to build me a temple nor recite a single ode to my ankles. I am only mortal and not worth the trouble."

*Trouble is the only currency you value, woman.* Phillip clenched his jaw in frustration but then forced himself to smile. If she wanted to punish him for confronting her in the garden, then so be it. But he wasn't going to abandon his course.

*Two can play at this game.*

"My poetry skills are a little rusty, Lady Wellcott. I would have to see the ankles in question before I could compose a few lines. Lift your skirts and let's see if I'm inspired."

The sound of crystal shattering to the floor as one of the footmen dropped his tray was rewarding but the flustered look of shock on Serena's face was like the gates of heaven giving way.

*I'm going to enjoy this, your ladyship.*

*And take you to school this time around.*

**

"Phillip!" Delilah caught him on the stairs. "Explain yourself! For in all the years that we have known each other, I have never heard you speak to a woman that way!"

"I apologize, dear cousin." Phillip turned back to address her, exhaustion forcing a sigh from his lips. "James has already given me an earful of disapproval. It has been such a long day and I…meant to do better."

"Lady Wellcott assured me that she wasn't offended but I cannot see how that is possible. What possessed you?" Delilah asked.

"Lady Wellcott appears to enjoy a bit of verbal sparring. I thought to play along. I'll admit I may have overshot the mark but if the lady has already opted not to complain, may I not get a pass? I would never wish to spoil an evening or anger a guest under your roof. I shall plead a headache or temporary insanity and tomorrow at breakfast, I swear I will be the most charming version of myself that not a single plate is lost."

Delilah smiled. "Very well. If no more of my best china or crystal is sacrificed, I do not see how I can refuse you."

"There's my saintly cousin," he said and leaned in to kiss her on the forehead. "Good night, Delilah."

"Good night, Phillip." She looked up at him, her eyes shining. "I am so glad you are here."

"Is…everything all right, cousin?"

"Yes. Yes, of course." She stepped back. "Go on and get some rest. I want to see that irresistible charm in the morning."

"Are you not coming up yourself?"

"Not yet," she said and took another step away from the staircase. "I have to have one last conversation with the housekeeper about getting some new tapers. The ones in the dining room were smoking so horribly I kept expecting a fire to break out."

Phillip shook his head in amazement. "How is it that women are so adept at the details? I never noticed but I leave it to your capable hands. Good night, cousin."

Phillip headed up the stairs aware that he would be lucky to reach his room before falling asleep. The long ride out had dented his physical reserves but the emotional upheaval of the return of Raven Wells had proven more than he'd bargained for.

And despite his assurances to Delilah, Phillip knew that while he might attempt a slightly more subtle approach in the company of others, he was not going to abandon a winning tactic. He would protect his family at any cost.

He opened his bedroom door and didn't bother with a lamp. He stripped out of his clothes and fell into the bed. *I'll keep you close, Raven. Hell, I'll keep you in my bed and naked if that is what it takes.*

It was his last thought before a dreamless void claimed him.

Chapter Six

Serena sailed into the dining room wearing a morning dress of pale blue with silver threads to echo her own eyes. It was a deliberately flattering selection and she reveled in the look of raw admiration it wrested from Phillip. The man did not look well-rested and her smile widened at the small hint of his discomfort.

"What a lovely breakfast setting!" she sighed as she took her place at the table. "I am positively famished!"

"Did you sleep well, Lady Wellcott?" Delilah asked.

"Like a babe," Serena replied. It was a bold-faced lie but Pepper was an alchemist at the dressing table and Serena knew that her face was as fresh as a rose to any observer. "There is nothing like the quiet of the country to provide such heavenly sleep. I am a new woman!"

Phillip choked a little on his eggs but she was the only one to notice.

"Have you plans for the day, Mrs. Osborne?" Serena asked sweetly.

"Not really. It promises to be so fine, I have asked the housekeeper to set up a shade tent in the garden where I might sit and sew. Dell is going to teach me a new embroidery stitch."

James smiled. "She is such a good girl and so…skilled. See that you pay close attention to her lessons, my dear."

Delilah's color changed to a ghostly hue and Serena leaned forward. "And you, Mr. Osborne? Will you hide inside today?"

"I have work to do but I am committed to riding out with my land manager. There is some nonsense about ditches but I've put it off too long." He shifted back after taking another muffin. "Sorry to leave you at loose ends, Cousin Phillip. But I wouldn't invite you along to what promises to be a spirit numbing afternoon of sheer boredom."

"I'm sure I can entertain myself." Phillip sipped his coffee and leaned back in his chair. "What of you, Lady Wellcott? Will you embroider in the garden and wile away the hours in female conversation?"

"I might." She selected a poached egg from a tray along with some toast. "There are worse ways to spend a day."

"Have you other hobbies or pursuits, Lady Wellcott? Do you not ride?" Phillip asked. "For I would love to take the horses out for a run across Southgate and show you the land. We can easily take advantage of the grand weather and spare you from confinement."

James sat up a little straighter, openly thrilled at Phillip's bold invitation to their guest. "Oh, yes! Do enjoy the day, Lady Wellcott! We have a horse or two with suitable temperaments for a gentle seat and Cousin Phillip is an excellent guide."

"Well," Serena began before glancing at Delilah. Clearly Mrs. Osborne was not going to offer the faintest whiff of resistance to the notion, and Serena let out a long sigh. She studied Phillip for a moment but the man was looking at her as innocently as a lamb.

*As if I would be fooled by that expression into forgetting what you are capable of Sir Phillip Warrick. You are trying to draw me out. For another confrontation? As if I would shy away from the chance? Idiot. You want to go out for a ride? Be careful what you wish for.*

"A ride sounds lovely," she conceded at last. "I only hope I can keep up, Sir Warrick."

"There! There!" James celebrated as if some great victory had been achieved. "Phillip will set a civilized pace, won't you, cousin?"

"Undoubtedly," Phillip said. "The lady couldn't be in better hands."

Serena had to ignore the urge to throw her toast in his face and instead smiled. "Aren't you sweet?"

Delilah's shoulders relaxed and Serena suspected she was relieved to see that Phillip was making an effort to amend for his poor behavior the night before.

*So long as Dell is in her company today, it should be safe to be away from the house for a few hours.*

"Believe it or not, Lady Wellcott, Sir Warrick was once one of the most charming young men in all of England!" James said with a flourish of his fork. "Of course, that was before he unexpectedly became 'Phillip the Porcupine'!"

"James!" Delilah chided softly. "Don't embarrass him so!"

"What? Come! Look at him! The man's been as dour as a vinegar vendor the last few years! I wished to compliment him on his cheer and simply make sure Lady Wellcott knew his potential to actually smile even if his social skills have grown a bit rusty." James put his fork down. "Can a man not make light conversation at his own breakfast table?"

Serena looked at Phillip who was staring daggers at James Osborne. "May I ask when he earned his quills?"

Phillip's gaze returned to her, a simmering anger in his eyes charging the air. "It is of no matter. I am as I have always been."

"What a liar!" James laughed. "It must be going on seven or eight years. No one's brave enough to hazard a good guess but whatever happened, it was memorable enough for him to turn into a badger with a grudge. He holes up in his estate and not a single season in London or house party. Hell, your friends wrote to ask if you had died and we'd forgotten to take out a column in the

Times!  That is," her host quickly began to amend his words, "until now!  Perhaps your lovely company has begun to amend his spirits, Lady Wellcott."

"One can only hope," she said softly then diverted to her plate.

"A woman's power should never be underestimated," Phillip intoned.

Delilah cleared her throat.  "Phillip is still the sweetest and most charming man and I say that we've poked at him enough for one day."  She smiled at her cousin and reached over to squeeze his wrist.  "Even just to avoid risking those quills."

Phillip's expression softened.  "I'll do my best not to injure anyone."

The rest of the meal unfolded without incident as Phillip asked James about the "nonsense of ditches" and the conversation diverted to farming and irrigation.  Serena tracked all of it, unwilling to be the first to retreat from the table.  The men discussed business and the profit of one kind of livestock versus another and without realizing it, Serena began to see him from a different vantage point.  Where James bemoaned the details and spoke of the local inhabitants as chattel, Phillip held a level view and never failed to demonstrate a strong respect for those who worked the land. Even as he confessed that most of his investments lay in industrial fields, Phillip proved that as a baron he was not blind to the sweat and labor that created the mortar between the bricks of his estate.

She tipped her head to one side. He was a man in his element and a peer. When she had first met him, she had seen only how handsome he was and while she'd thought him clever and kind, there had been a blinding madness in the emotions of a young girl falling in love for the first time. She would have been quick to bleat poetry about his form and face, hungering endlessly for his kisses but it would never have occurred to her seventeen year old self to inquire into his financial skills or approaches to management.

Sir Phillip Warrick's gaze shifted back to her and her cheeks warmed to be caught staring at him. Holding her place to prove indifference was a tactic she immediately abandoned. Serena stood abruptly. "If you will excuse me."

The men shifted to stand politely at her retreat.

"Until this afternoon, Lady Wellcott," Phillip said. "I *so* look forward to it."

"As do I."

She sailed from the room concentrating only on the even brisk sound of her heels against the wooden floors. And the fury of forgetting herself in front of him. Now there was nothing to do but head upstairs and give Pepper the news that she would need to brush out her riding costume.


James' stables yielded a biddable mare for Lady Wellcott and Phillip rode his own stallion. There was little conversation to be had as they left the stable yard at a brisk pace that evolved into a breathless gallop across the fields. Phillip wasn't sure what they were racing against but neither wanted to be the first to yield. He kept a close eye on her as he noted that she was not very comfortable on horseback but Lady Serena Wellcott was fearless.

*If courage were the measure of a rider, there would be no catching her.*

Eventually it was the stamina of their mounts that forced them to relent and out of necessity, they ended up in a gentle walk along a lane beside a wooded grove cut with a stream.

A thousand thoughts clamored for expression but Phillip finally settled on attempting to hold out an olive branch. "I was a fool to swallow Trent's poison."

"Phillip." She pulled up on the reins of her horse, and he did the same. "As easy as it would be to throw that back in your face, I am tired of the taste of acid in my mouth when I look at you much less speak of our mutual past. Tomorrow is soon enough to loathe the very sight of you. But today, the sun is shining and I am bone-tired. Today I want to pretend that you are simply Phillip Warrick, cousin to a friend and that there is nothing beyond this moment. No ugly past, no threatening future, just this moment. Can we do that?"

"You always did have a talent for surprising me, Lady Wellcott." He nodded slowly, wary of such an unexpected truce. "I don't see why we couldn't try."

"Thank you." She let out a sigh. "Do you mind if we walk for a bit? I am not so practiced in the saddle and feel the need to stretch my legs."

He dismounted quickly and chivalrously moved to help her do the same. "A walk sounds refreshing."

"Yes." She slid from her saddle without taking his hand, refusing to allow him to touch her. Serena gathered up the reins of her mare and they began to make their way down the lane. "I was never much of a horsewoman."

"No?" Phillip smiled. "It's strange, but I find it hard to imagine that you aren't spectacular at everything you do, Lady Wellcott."

"It's an art to leave you with that impression." She untied the scarf at her throat and allowed it to trail from one hand. "But too much effort today."

"Can I ask what has changed?"

She shook her head. "The rights and privileges of a woman are few and far between but being changeable and mysterious must be universally understood."

"Look, there's a brook just there. Let's bring the horses down for a drink and take our respite there." Phillip said, politely taking note that the lady was limping slightly.

She yielded to his suggestion and they tied off the horses before finding a comfortable place to sit by the music of the brook.

He waited for her to speak and then gave in to the balm of being in the presence of a woman he had once loved. Phillip glanced over to study her, so very real and alive it took his breath away all over again. For wasn't this the dream he'd had? To have her by his side? To have the perfume of her hair on the breeze and Raven within reach?

She looked back at him, openly accepting his study. "Is it a pleasing picture?"

He nodded. "You are the most beautiful woman I have ever known. I don't see a thousand centuries changing that fact."

"A thousand centuries," she echoed and began to pull off her boots and stockings. "A pretty phrase, sir." She looked up at him. "Where do men learn to say such pretty things?"

"University?" he said with a wry smile.

Raven laughed. "Ah! I should have guessed!"

"I often wished I'd paid more attention to the classics. If only it meant being able to keep up with your wit and intelligence, Raven."

She stiffened. "Don't use that name."

"I'm sorry. Lady Wellcott," he amended softly. "Truly sorry."

"Apology accepted." She stood from their perch and tucked the greater length of her riding skirt around her waist in a clever knot that raised the garment up to her knees revealing the ankles he'd so mockingly offered to worship. "I'm going to walk into the shallows."

He held out his elbow to steady her and without a word, she accepted his arm. Phillip kept his boots on, uncaring of the state of his pants as Raven wobbled into the ice cold water and giggled at the sensation of smooth rocks and silky sand against her bare feet.

"When I was young, I used to pretend that I was a water nymph," she confessed. "I imagined that I could dance on the glassy surface of any body of water so long as my heart was pure. Isn't that silly?"

He nodded, not trusting his own voice. Because it didn't sound silly at all when she said it with a faint echo of forgotten innocence in her eyes and merriment altering her so much that it made his chest ache.

She released his arm to balance on a rock above the babbling flow at the brook's deepest point, her hands outstretched as if she were about to take flight. "What do you think, Warrick? Is it too late to make my petition to Queen Maeb and see if she'll have me?" she teased.

He stepped carefully onto a rock furthest out to help steady her if she needed it and laughter ceased. "It is never too late."

"How strange that now you are the one who sounds like an optimist and I am the pragmatic cynic." She put her arms down and the knot holding her skirts loosened to let her hem fall to skim the water's surface. She was transformed into a feminine creature that appeared to stand on the water itself, her eyes as cold as the brook at her feet. But she was still human, still full of fire and tempestuous impulses that made him long to warm his soul and hold her close.

"Raven, please! I—"

Her expression twisted in fury. "I bid you not to call me that! You are *never* to use that name! I was a fool to indulge myself like this! To think that it was even possible to escape— Never again!"

"Wait."

"Wait? Wait for what, Phillip? For reason to return? Well, for that you need wait no longer." She lifted the hem of her skirts and moved skillfully from rock to rock heading toward the bank.

Phillip turned on his precarious perch. "We don't need to be enemies, Lady Wellcott."

"No? What are we to be? Friends? Acquaintances?" She dipped her chin down to look at him through her lashes. "Lovers?"

His gut twisted at the word. "Rav—I meant—"

"Thank you for indulging me in an afternoon of fantasy and daydreams. But I think it is time we both returned to the real world."

"Do you hate all men, Lady Wellcott?"

"No, of course not. I am not an unreasonable woman." She recrossed the stones effortlessly to stand before him on the precarious bridge of stones. "I hate men who lie, or abuse others, or think that they live apart from the moral laws of this world. I hate men who are self-important or pompous or arrogant. I hate cruel men and men who wallow in ignorance clinging to it as if their twisted views formed plated armor to make them righteous and invincible."

Lady Wellcott tipped her head to one side and froze him with a seductive smile that did not match her speech, flooding him with foreboding. "But what I loathe above all are men who speak of love, and tenderly promise their hearts when all the while they have no heart to give."

It wasn't that she pushed him with any great force, but it was a quick lightning strike against the center of his chest; and it was all that was needed. Phillip's arms pinwheeled to try to keep his balance before he lost the struggle to fall back into the icy cold stream to land on his backside with an ungrateful splash.

"God…. Damn it, woman!" Phillip sputtered as he stood up from the shin deep water, his clothes soaked in a punishing grip on his body. "I thought you didn't want to fight today?"

She laughed as she made her way with light steps to the safety of the grassy bank to fetch her boots and stockings. "How many times must I tell you that it is a woman's right to be changeable? But I thank you for such a refreshing ride, sir. I cannot remember the last time I laughed out loud."

"Damn it!"

She retrieved her horse just in time to watch him take an unfortunate step onto a mossy rock that gave way to dump him back into the brook. As she mounted her horse, Raven began to truly laugh, uncontrollable peals of merriment at the delicious sight of Phillip Warrick sputtering and cursing from an ignoble seat in the water. "Priceless. Thank you, sir. Priceless!"

She spurred her mount and was off, reveling in the moment.

*Who knew that joy and a taste of satisfaction could come with a splash?*

**

Serena walked up the steps of Southgate, as merry as a child on holiday.

"Did you have a pleasant ride?" Delilah asked before her eyes widened at the sight of Serena's wet skirts and the boots she held in her hands. "Oh! Did you fall?"

"No." Serena shifted to step around her and start toward the staircase.

"Lady Wellcott?"

Serena stopped and faced her hostess. "Yes?"

"What is it between you and my cousin? I cannot help but notice the strange tension that lingers whenever you are in the same room and," Delilah cleared her throat. "Wasn't he with you on your ride today?"

"He was." Serena forced a smile. "Though he fared worse, I am sorry to say. As for the other question, I cannot say."

"Cannot?"

Serena shook her head. "Of all the men on this earth, Phillip Warrick is—don't worry, friend. He will remain unbruised and I have no interest in sparring any longer. I am here for the matter at hand not the distractions of Sir Phillip Warrick. Now, I shall change quickly for tea time and see you shortly." She picked up her skirts to continue back up the stairs while a bemused Delilah watched her go with a smile.

It was a soggy miserable ride back. The day was warm but not enough to prove a relief from the layers of soaking clothes that chafed against his skin and fueled his anger. Setting out, he'd been prepared for more slicing banter, quiet venom or—hell, he'd been ready for anything!

*Queen Maeb! Water nymphs! What a load of tripe! And I'm standing there with my mouth open begging her for more!*

The actress had gained in her skills. Like a chameleon, she shifted to her own advantage and without warning, she'd dropped the reserved mantle of a refined lady and walked into the water like a country maid. And God, he'd had no defenses against her in that guise.

Time had melted away and he'd lost his place in the fight.

*Where was the harridan? Where was the terrifying creature who taunted him in the garden and scoffed at his threats?*

*That* woman he'd have rebuffed with ease.

By the time he reached the stables, every bone in his body was aching with the damp. Not a single groomsman made one comment as to the state of his clothes and Phillip stalked into the house to change.

The look on the valet's face when he picked up the ruin of Phillip's riding boots spoke volumes but the transition to dry clothes suitable for the afternoon was made without a single word. He selected a soft brushed light wool coat of green and eyed his reflection with critical eyes. The lines were good and his cravat was tied with a casual style he favored. He waved away any offer of a pomade and decided that he would pass any inspection the witch cared to make.

He headed out only to find James waiting at the bottom of the stairs. "I knew you were back but then one had only to follow the trail of your watery footsteps on my carpets…"

"I didn't know you to be so fastidious about the state of your floors, James." Phillip readjusted the buttons of his shirt at his wrists. "I'd have stripped naked and left my wet things on your doorstep, but I didn't want to traumatize the modest sensibilities of your staff."

"What happened out there?" James demanded. "Delilah said that Lady Wellcott returned some time ago and *alone*! What the hell are you doing?"

"I am coming down to have a cup of tea in the drawing room."

"That's not what I meant and well you know it! What are you doing with Lady Wellcott? She's worth a hundred thousand pounds or more! I've heard tell she has a purse so deep she could finance a small war if she had a mind to!"

Phillip crossed his arms, the memory of an icy bath a bit too recent not to add to the sting of the present fight. "Well, imagine that! Should we warn any neighboring countries to beef up their defenses before it's too late?"

"If you mean to seduce this woman and win her, I hardly think hurling yourself into creeks is the way to her heart, Phillip."

"I do not mean to seduce this woman, James. I do not mean to win anything to do with that creature! She is the last woman on this earth I would touch and you're a fool to push me! Lady Serena Wellcott is—"

"Standing just behind you?" Serena's voice cut him off, her tone full of amusement. "Pardon me for interrupting but I offered to be the one to tell you that tea was being served in the garden. Mrs. Osborne thought it would be a lovely surprise for you both."

*Shit.*

James nodded stiffly. "Yes. A lovely surprise. We shall *both* be right there to join you ladies." He gave Phillip a look full of icy reproach. "Won't we, Phillip?"

"Oh, I am living to have tea in the garden." Phillip kept his voice level but sarcasm bled through to betray him.

She rewarded him with a smile to make a lesser man bay at her feet. "Imagine that, Sir Warrick! Such achievable dreams! Aren't you wise!"

She left both men at the bottom of the stairs and Phillip's hands fisted useless at his side.

*If I don't strangle you, Raven Wells, before the week is out, you will have Providence alone to thank for it.*


The tea was a disaster. James, for all his proclamations that both men would endure the challenge ahead, did not have the courage to even sit down. His nerves failed him at the sight of the lady that Phillip had so roundly insulted. James brusquely kissed the top of his wife's head with a mumbled apology about the demands of his ledgers before striding back to the safety of the house.

Phillip took a contrite seat across from the ladies, made a silent prayer for a sudden rainstorm and then glanced up at the betrayal of a clear blue sky.

*Spring in England. It should be damn well raining all the time…*

"Isn't this a nice surprise?" Phillip tried to smile. "Tea in the garden."

Delilah gave him a puzzled look. "Come now! I know I have failed to provide jugglers, but surely this is not such a sad scene."

"It is truly elegant," Lady Wellcott said quietly. "Nothing can match the splendor of nature for a dining room. Don't you think so, Sir Warrick? A long table set with silver under a grand tree…"

"Until you find a bug in your drink." He was being a surly child and he knew it. She was deliberately evoking memories of their shared past and he was in no mood to indulge her. And immediately regretted his pout when Lady Wellcott set down her tea cup.

"Pardon me, Mrs. Osborne. I am suddenly unwell but I know your cousin will entertain you well enough. He is such *lively* company."

She stood and left them before Delilah could compose a protest and James' flush of relief died quickly when he was left with an openly distressed Delilah Osborne.

"Phillip! You promised! You swore you would be your most charming self with Lady Wellcott! But…this?" She placed her hands on the table. "What flavor of insanity has seized you?"

"The horse ride didn't go well. I fell in the brook. I'm— feeling out of sorts."

The snap of anger in her eyes didn't soften as he'd hoped at the mention of his mishap—and that was the moment when Phillip realized that he was truly out of his cousin's good graces.

"Looking at you I would say that the only injury you suffered was your pride."

"Delilah, in all honesty, I should tell you before your husband relishes his chance that I may have—Lady Wellcott overheard me just before we walked out to join you in a candid conversation with James regarding my…reluctance to play the suitor."

Delilah's eyes widened. "Reluctance?"

"More like repugnance. It wasn't my best moment."

"Phillip," she began and then stopped taking a slow breath. Phillip braced himself for a scathing lecture but instead felt the lash of guilt he couldn't avoid when Delilah's eyes filled with tears. "I…have already entreated you to be kind. What else can I do?"

"Delilah." Words failed him.

"Lady Wellcott is very—very important to me, Phillip. If you drive her off…"

"I don't wish to drive her off. Though," he sighed. "That's not to say I won't be relieved and happy to see her trunks on your front steps. I'm so sorry, Delilah."

Tears overflowed in a demonstration of genuine distress and Phillip was defeated. "You are *not* sorry! But if ever you loved me, Phillip Warrick, you will cease acting like a jilted and ridiculous bully in Lady Wellcott's presence! You will...oh God!"

Delilah became too upset to plead her case and Phillip instinctively came around the table to kneel next to her and take her into his arms. He closed his eyes helplessly as she cried against his shoulder.

"Delilah! I will make amends, I swear it! Lady Wellcott will—I would leave before it came to such a thing and..." He reached up to stroke her hair as he had when she had been a child lamenting a spoiled dress. "Delilah, what is this? What distresses you so? Why do I have the feeling that there is more to this?"

Delilah shook her head and pushed away from the comfort of his arms. "Nothing matters beyond the peace of this visit, Phillip. Please! Behave! And..." She wiped her eyes with the handkerchief he held out to her. "And I shall write Grandmama and sing your praises."

Phillip raised one eyebrow at Delilah's sweet nature that had defaulted to offer him a reward before resorting to the more obvious choice to threaten a thunderous report to his Great Aunt Bella. "I will do everything in my power to earn a glowing account of myself."

"You will? Truly?"

He nodded solemnly. "Honor demands it. I cannot have my favorite cousin thinking me a ridiculous bully."

"A *jilted* and ridiculous bully," she echoed, a trace of humor finally returning to her.

"Terrible choice of words." He sighed. "I will have to do everything in my power to get you to never repeat it again."

She smiled. "See that you do!" Delilah pat his hand as one would a senile old man's. "Now, sit down and have tea with me, Cousin Phillip. I cannot face Mrs. Watson if I put her to all this trouble and not a single cup was enjoyed."

Phillip returned to his chair. "I will leave your housekeeper's happiness to you after this. I can only manage so many tasks, Delilah, and pleasing Lady Wellcott is an assignment I suspect Hercules would have run from..." Delilah gasped but he went on quickly, "And a trial I shall cheerfully overcome. I am honor bound."

*Honor bound and hell bent.*

Chapter Seven

She pleaded a headache and had a dinner tray sent up that night,

fully aware that Phillip would be blamed for her absence and suffer

a miserable evening to cap off his miserable day. Pepper took in a

full accounting of the lectures he'd endured down in the servants'

hallways and conveyed the best tidbits to her mistress.

"It's a roasting, poor man! Mr. Osborne's furious to think

Sir Warrick's insulted you beyond recovery." Pepper giggled.

"Not a whisper of a defense, until Mrs. Osborne finally had to end

it to keep her heart from breaking."

"Mrs. Osborne does not have the stomach for conflict."

Serena noted and took a bite of beef from her plate. "Serves Phillip

right. I'll take a tray for breakfast, as well. That should round out

the lesson nicely."

"If he survives until lunch, I don't think that man will be inviting you out for a ride ever again!" Pepper said and then helped herself to a piece of bread from her mistress's tray.

"Good! I am still sore from making a fool of myself. They say pride goeth before the fall, but I swear I would feel better if I had fallen off that animal instead of galloping around attempting to look like Diana of the Hunt to prove some obscure point."

Pepper shook her head. "You don't need to prove a thing to that man."

"No. You're right." She held out a bite of candied beets, aware that it was Pepper's favorite. "It is time to expend our energy where it will do the most good."

Pepper took the fork and the women sat across from each other, merrily sharing the tray and falling into the easy conversation of dearest friends before Serena began to make notes of the names of all the maids and manservants, gathering the intelligence of the house like a general preparing for the battle ahead.

Pepper was an invaluable scout, adding crisp details to paint in personalities and sketch out the routines and timing for Southgate and a Mr. James Osborne.

They worked into the late hours of the night and then as Pepper headed off to bed in the servants' quarters, Serena dropped all her notes into the fire. For the Black Rose never left a written trace of their work...

And Lady Serena Wellcott was too clever to forget anything.

**

The next afternoon, she took a leisurely stroll in the gardens and simply waited. She knew it wouldn't be long before the eyes of the house alerted Sir Warrick to her solitary presence and pushed him out the door to apologize.

For amusement, she began to count to a hundred and before she'd reached the sixties, he was there. His expression hardly contrite but instead surly, a sure sign that he hadn't come entirely of his own volition.

Serena smiled. It was impossible not to enjoy the moment. "Oh, Sir Warrick! What a delight to find you here—and so unexpectedly!"

"Do try to hide your glee, Lady Wellcott." Phillip let out a long slow breath. "I think you're the only one I know who can arrange it so that not only do I get pushed into an icy stream, you have them all convinced that I am at fault and somehow owe you an apology!"

"Oh," she looked at him through a flirtatious batting of her eyelashes. "You do not wish to apologize, Sir Warrick? Are you sure?"

"I do wish to apologize." The hard edge of frustration disappeared from his voice and the sincere tone jolted her nerves. "Where should I begin?"

Her breath caught in her throat. "Wherever you wish."

He nodded. "Delilah is very dear to me. I've roared and fussed at you and…it comes to naught. I am sorry, Lady Wellcott. Yesterday, you pleaded for a day's respite but you deserve more than a single day."

"And what do I deserve then, Sir Warrick?"

"It is exhausting to hate and regret is a disease that destroys everything in its path. I should know, Lady Wellcott. I have wasted years…" He let out a slow breath and then put his hands behind his back. "I apologize for distressing you during your country holiday. I apologize for spoiling Delilah's peace of mind and I hope that you will not punish her for my boarish behavior by leaving."

"So, this apology is for Delilah?" He'd missed the mark in so many ways, it astonished her but his sincere concern for his cousin was not without merit. Delilah was worried that Phillip would send her packing. Phillip had promised to ask her not to leave and to "apologize". And God help him, the man had done just that.

Just that and not one thing more.

She shook her head, a sad smile crossing her features. "Aren't you dear?" She stepped closer, indulging in his presence. "What a puzzle."

"I want a truce, Lady Wellcott. For Delilah's sake."

"For her sake, I grant it. I shall go even further, Sir Warrick. Would you like me to smile and laugh at your jests, sigh at your heroic stories and ensure that no one in that house believes that I am not completely charmed by your person? How does that sound?"

"Like some kind of deadly trap," he admitted quietly.

"It is."

"God, woman. I think I've demonstrated my good intentions, have I not? Mercy."

She took an unsteady move away from him, pain lashing through her chest. *Mercy. A little word. A little word. Banished. I banished it from myself. Even when the scales are balanced, mercy has no weight.*

"I cannot give you what I do not have, Sir Warrick. I cannot provide something I know to be a lie in this world. What mercy? What mercy do you understand? Tell me what mercy looks like and I will drown you in it—I will choke you with it." She shook her head. "Assure your cousin that I will not abandon her. But *you* are nothing to me. The only thing you have *demonstrated* is how blind you are. You are like a madman apologizing for dancing after burning a house down with children inside! You disgust me."

"God damn it! I do not *owe* you an apology, woman."

Her eyes widened and she stared at him in shock. "No? Truly? For anything?"

Phillip stubbornly crossed his arms. "I've paid for my sins already. I don't have to make an accounting to you. Our parting was rude, I'll grant you that and I've regretted my behavior but—it was not unprovoked, Lady Wellcott."

Serena's gaze narrowed and she deliberately shifted to make sure that he was blocking a view of her from most of the windows. "I didn't think to think less of you, Phillip. But thank you."

"Do you really hate me so much?" he asked softly.

She held very still—as enigmatic as the stones of the earth. "I? Hate you?" Raven's breath caught in her throat. *Hate.* It was a tidy word that felt misplaced from the raging fire of loathing and longing that warred inside of her. "I do not have to confide my feelings to you, Phillip. You have no right to any confessions of my interior landscape, no glimpse of any part of my soul that I do not wish you to see." She began to walk back toward the house her head held high.

Phillip held his ground but stopped her in her tracks when he spoke. "Tell me what you want, Serena. An abject apology for failing to be the dupe you and Trent wanted? Shall I write you a cheque? To compensate you for your wounds? Would that assuage your dislike? Or do those offers only solidify your opinions of my worthlessness?"

Serena pivoted back to face him. "I will break my own rule and tell you exactly what I want, Phillip." She smiled, a thing so beautiful it frightened him because the grey in her eyes was so cold his bones felt brittle to see them. "I want victory. I want to break you in every way it is possible to break a man. And when you are on your knees, only then I think I will be whole. I will bury what is left of Raven in your ashes and you, Phillip, you can make your peace with the Devil however you wish."

"And now what? Do you expect me to volunteer to stay? To stand by and participate as a victim and be broken?"

"Of course not." She closed the distance between them slowly, a strange seductive sway in her hips hypnotizing him into holding his ground.

*God. This is how a bird feels when a cobra spreads its hood and begins to dance.*

"Fight me, Phillip. Defend your ground. Prove your manhood and your bravery." Her lips pressed into a pout that made his cock irrationally hard. "You're not afraid of a weak fragile woman. You'll not run for all the world to mock and pity. Strike me down, in any way you can. Stop me. Hurt me. Do. Your. Worst."

"You're insane, Serena."

She shook her head. "I am not insane. I am swimming in reason. But I dare you, Phillip. For I tell you, I will do my worst and I will win this game."

"The game ended seven years ago."

"If you say so, Sir Warrick."

"Put your claws away, Lady Wellcott. We both made mistakes that fateful spring."

She was close enough to kiss and he briefly considered it. Her countenance softened.

"Yes. Tell me. I know my own sins. But what would you say was your worst misstep, Phillip?"

"Besides accepting Lord Trent's invitation to come to Oakwell Manor?"

She shook her head. "No. That wasn't it."

"Wasn't it?" he scoffed.

"No."

"What then?"

"Could it be that you never asked yourself why he would send that letter?"

Phillip's brow furrowed. "Wasn't it obvious? So that he could crow over his achievement in humiliating me."

"Why? Why send it when his threat to expose your foolish error to the papers would have done the work and more?" She sighed. "If I was his creature, why admit it so openly? Why give it away?"

"I don't understand. He meant for me to read it after we were married. It wouldn't have mattered to—"

"Ah! But you could have annulled the union based on the fraud or your belief in my besmirched character. You had written proof of his scheme in your possession to see to it all."

"I…had no such proof after I gave the letter to you."

She smiled. "An act I have neglected to thank you for."

"So tell me again, what was my great mistake, Lady Wellcott?"

"Yes. One last favor for old time's sake. You must learn to look at things from a different vantage point, Sir Warrick. For then, it might occur to you that the best revenge might have been robbing you of the woman you appeared to love. If Trent wanted to hurt you, which clearly he did, then what better way than vomiting lies about your bride and destroying your peace of mind?"

"But...I..."

"Your greatest mistake was that no matter how duplicitous the earl proved he was, you still relied on his words and submitted your wits. You saw the word 'whore' and your pride did the rest. You muted your own heart and every experience that defied his lies when it came to me. You had my innocence as a gift I gave freely only because I loved you. I was fearless! I cared nothing for my reputation or honor. I only knew that you were the man I wanted above all else. But you—you're a man defined by pride and vanity. You valued your honor more than anything—more than love, more than me.  As he knew you would.  Do you still think I hate you, Sir Warrick?"  She stepped back, whipped open her fan and curtsied.  "Well, what a lovely afternoon's interlude.  If you'll excuse me, I'm fatigued and in need of a headache powder."

She left without another word and Phillip sat down hard on a garden bench, his entire body rendered numb.

*I'd never looked at it like that.*

*Damn it.*

Chapter Eight

She rang the bell and waited for Pepper, pacing and walking off the fog of her emotions. Phillip Warrick's presence was so much more potent than she'd allowed herself to remember. God help her, in the middle of all those invectives, she'd nearly begged him to kiss her again—came within a breath of pressing her body against his.

Her desire for him had not faded.

Worse, it had grown over time.

Pepper came through the door with a peppermint striped satin skirt draped over her arm. "Are you changing early for tea?"

Raven shook her head. "I want a bath. Have it drawn and then I'll send a note to Delilah that I won't come down until dinner tonight."

"A difficult afternoon then?" Pepper asked shyly. "I may have been watching from the windows but even downstairs there's word that Sir Warrick was seen storming from the garden toward the stables not long ago."

"Fascinating." Serena crossed her arms but her pacing halted. "I'll wear the gold tonight at dinner."

"The gold?" Pepper hung the skirt in the wardrobe. "Making a statement are we?"

"We are." Serena pressed her cool fingertips against her temples. "A declaration of war."

"I have never seen anyone affect you like this."

"It is no matter. I've frightened him off and he will stay out of my way after this." She began to pull the pins from her hair to drop them on the table. "I abandoned subtlety but it's better this way. He'll lick his wounds and be on his best behavior from now on. Especially since he has no ally in his family. Mr. Osborne is too socially ambitious and greedy not to howl if I miss another meal and point at Sir Warrick as the cause. Phillip dare not make any more scenes and I will be free to concentrate on our true purpose here."

"Frightened him off?" Pepper shook her head in disbelief but began to retreat to arrange the bath. "I may not know men as well as you, but by the looks of his face when you marched off from him in the garden…"

"Yes?"

Pepper shrugged. "Didn't look like terror to me. Looked like he'd just lost something precious to him."

Serena turned away, unwilling to hear more. "Good! He needs to be acquainted with loss for if I have my way, it is all that man will ever know."

Pepper closed the door behind her and Serena laid her head on her hands and let the tears come.

\*\*\*

Phillip rode hard as if he could outrun himself.

He didn't want to give her words credence, didn't want to believe anything she said. Because if she weren't lying then it was possible for him to drown in his own guilt. The buried memories resurrected but with new force and a strange new power.

The agony of Trent's accusations had blinded him to any study of them. Like a fatal wound, his spirit had instinctively shrunk from pressing his fingers into the rift. He'd spent all this time savaging Raven's memory for her part in the earl's petty revenge against him.

Now there was no avoiding it.

He abandoned his ride, unwilling to risk the animal in a selfish tantrum of his own making. The stallion's sides were coated with sweat, lather dripping from his mouth and Phillip cursed his thoughtless cruelty. He dismounted to walk the horse, cooling him off gradually to preserve his legs.

*What if I am at heart nothing but a cruel and thoughtless man?*

He drank it in. He let the teeth of it cut into his skin. He'd loved her. He'd always thought he'd once loved her completely and without reserve. He'd fallen in love with a girl who had been as wild as a colt and sweetly eager for his every touch. He'd said that despite her betrayal, he had been the better man for going back and searching for her.

He'd comforted himself with the idea that he would have taken her back despite her flaws. Despite the failings in her character that swarmed his senses and made him forget everything else but having her.

Despite them.

Despite everything. And nothing.

He'd searched for her for months but there had been no sign of her and his fear of scandal had robbed him of allies. There'd been no one he could talk to for fear of admitting to her murder.

Then he'd grieved because she was surely dead.

The wound had deepened and never healed.

He had never reached for it because a man couldn't survive it if he kept looking at the blood on his hands. Phillip had survived as one last flimsy stand against Trent, as if to say, "I live therefore I am not defeated."

As if he could ward off failure by insisting on breathing.

Lady Serena Wellcott looked through him with those smoke colored eyes that did not shy away from carnage. Lady Serena Wellcott simmered and bristled and then leaned in close to bewitch him with her beauty and whispered, "That blood on your hands is mine."

If she were as innocent as she claimed all those years ago, then he couldn't retreat. Every wrong he'd committed was now tempered in a renewed forge with every cutting accusation she made.

Lady Serena Wellcott taunted him about being blind.

And he was.

But no longer.

There had to be a way back.

He'd stopped looking for Raven Wells years ago. But as Phillip turned back toward the house, he was a man inspired. He would find her again and he would heal the wounds of the past.

Phillip didn't knock before he came into her room, winded from his return. He dispensed with all the pleasantries as quickly as a man tossing aside useless trash. Just like the first time he'd seen her in the salon downstairs, he had mud on his coat and clothes and Phillip decided that it was fitting.

But when he realized that Lady Wellcott was reclining in a large copper bath in the midst of the room, his momentum faltered.

"Get out!" she screeched in surprise.

He shook his head. "You don't hate me."

"Don't I?"

"The fire and venom you throw at me betrays you, Lady Wellcott. Love and hate are sides of the same coin." He knelt next to the bath, forcing himself to look only at her face. "I know because I am in the same inescapable bind. For better or worse, there has not been a single woman since you. Not one who has occupied my dreams, distracted me beyond a passing conversation. Not one who ever came close to comparing to the shadow of you. I have refused to say your name aloud. Seven years, Lady Wellcott. What would you call that? Abject hatred? I am no longer so sure of that."

She shook her head slowly, as if dazed.

"And what of you, Lady Wellcott? Seven years and I have the feeling that you never forgot me either but that you also have done everything in your power to deny that I ever existed. For I wasn't in hiding. If you'd wanted to confront me publicly or see to my destruction, then why wait?"

"Perhaps I was biding my time until the right moment."

"Here I am then. Tell me you hate me if you can."

"Get out." It was a whisper this time, a breathless powerless thing.

"You want to destroy me, Lady Wellcott? I wonder if you haven't already accomplished it. You want me to fight you? I won't. I am…a fool. But I have decided that if there is redemption to be had in this world, then you alone can provide it. I don't know what tortures you have in mind but you were right in guessing that I wouldn't run. I will never run from you again. Do what you must. But I am going to stand my ground and earn my way back to my humanity."

"I hate you. Go regain your humanity somewhere else and leave me to my bath, Warrick."

He shook his head. "You win. Do you hear me? Scream the house in and tell Delilah what an ass I am. I'll recount every sin and suffer any humiliation you dictate but I—I am yours, woman."

"All well and good," she whispered. "But I shall never be yours. *Never.*"

God help her, after so much time of wanting the man at her mercy, she was at a loss. If his 'surrender' was sincere, then here was the moment when she crushed him, cried out for the servants and had him banished from his beloved cousin's home—but she couldn't. Because the notion of sending him off, of never seeing him again or touching him had become a strange torture for her; and it was a weak excuse to alter her plans. "I should bed you just to break your heart, Phillip. I should indulge myself for selfish wicked pleasure alone, to have my fill of you before I cast you off on some roadside, you bastard. What do you think of that?"

His eyes were sad but there was also a new heat there. "Break me then. Break me if you can."

"Phillip."

He leaned over, gripping both sides of the tub to effectively hold her in place, but there was nothing menacing in his stance. "Serena."

She gasped at the sound of her chosen name on his lips. Her head tipped back as he loomed over and across her, and Serena knew no fear. She reached up with her arms to encircle his neck and drew his lips down to hers, in an invitation of demand and desire.

At the first touch of the rough silk of his lips to hers, something in her unleashed with a speed and fury that ended thought. It was a hunger so sharp it stole her breath and made her cry out. *Oh, god. Too long. It's been too long!*

The kiss deepened, her mouth opening quickly to taste him, to use all her senses to drink him in. His mouth was a pocket of warm velvet and he met every move she made with his own, equally hungry, until she sighed and groaned at the delicious surrender of her body to his. Electric flares of heat shimmered down her spine to pool between her hips, her arousal so fierce she could feel the molten slick begin to escape her body and slide down her inner thighs.

"Phillip, hurry."

"No." He shook his head, giving her a lazy grin. "If I remember it right, all we ever did was rush. I have waited seven years for this and if you think I'm going to race you to the finish; you have lost your mind, woman."

"Really? My maid will be back to get me out of this bath, Phillip Warrick, and that will be that."

"To Hell with it! We'll go slow next time."

Her eyes widened at the blatant confidence the words 'next time' betrayed but there was no time to do more than smile before he was kissing her again, this time with an urgency that matched her own.

For Phillip, she was a water nymph after all. Wet warm hands gripped his collar and began to send rivulets of soapy water down his back, anointing his skin with every caress. His hands roamed over the inviting landscape that was all woman.

Kissing her was ambrosia, but her breasts beckoned for his attention and Phillip growled at the age old dilemma of realizing that it wasn't possible to taste all of her at once. It was simply a problem that demanded a man to patiently sample what he could. She was curvier, her appeal so potent just the sight of her body was pushing him over the edge. She was still a creature of lean lines but the reality of Raven surpassed his dreams. His hands were filled with the ample weight of her breasts and she arched and writhed into his every touch, increasing the pressure of his fingers, sliding her body into his hands, urging him on.

He teetered on the edge of the tub's rolled metal sides and the fight for freedom from buttons and cloth was on. It was that or accept that he was about to climb into the copper bath fully clothed.

She laughed at his struggles, trailing her mouth down his bared chest, the low feminine vibration of it making his cock so hard it nearly pained him.

It was nearly a lost cause as he momentarily considered just diving in but within seconds, his clothes ended up in a soggy pile on the floor next to the bath. He lifted her up out of the bath to hold against him before he stepped into the water. The contact between them was electric. Slippery friction yielded ripple after ripple of pleasure and when she wrapped her bare legs around his waist, the silk hot folds of her sex meeting the rock hard jutting tower of his erection.

"Look into my eyes, Serena."

She complied, locking her focus onto his face and absorbing the shift in his expression as he slowly entered her, lowering her masterfully downward until her tight slick channel enveloped his flesh, stretching to accommodate him, squeezing him to pull him in deeper and deeper until they were one.

She held her breath and savored it, holding very still but she was too impatient to draw the moment out. He knelt slowly in the bath until they were in the water up to their waists. He closed his eyes and Serena smiled with a sigh. She wriggled her hips to heighten the sensation of fullness and was surprised when he gripped her waist to stop her.

"Don't move. I…need a moment."

She leaned in to kiss his throat and then leveraged herself up using her thighs over his to reach the sensitive shell of his ear. She flicked it with her tongue and then playfully bit his earlobe. "I know what I need, Phillip, and it does not involve sitting here quietly until the water grows cold."

He groaned as she planted a hot kiss in the sensitive well behind his ear. "As you wish, wicked lady."

The bath was not necessarily built for what he had in mind but Phillip wasn't about to let a minor inconvenience get in the way. He shifted back until he was kneeling at the farthest end of the tub to give her room. "Lean back."

Her eyes fluttered with a question at the command but she obeyed him readily, eager for the movement she craved. With her legs wrapped around his waist for ballast, he slowly lowered her back until she was floating on the surface of the water. Serena smiled in delight as she realized that there was no possibility of her face slipping beneath the water, but instead that the warmth held up her—the water, her natural buoyancy and the fact that she was completely impaled by Phillip Warrick's throbbing manhood.

At the first withdrawal and thrust, the world fell away.

She couldn't touch him, could do nothing more than grip the rolled metal sides of the tub and ride the sensations of being at his mercy. Serena unhooked her ankles from behind his back to press the soles of her feet against the back rim of the tub for more leverage, deepening the contact and pushing out to extend the length of his strokes. He kept one arm wrapped around her hips, his hand splayed at her lower back to guide her body but the other hand was free to explore, to tease and to touch her as he wished.

She boldly caught his wrist to show him where her desires demanded his attention. He slipped his fingers downward to the small hardened nub of her clit, his touch dancing over it, rubbing her in concert with the press of his hips until she couldn't hold back. Her hips bucked and lifted as an arc of white hot tension exploded through her frame. She grit her teeth to keep from crying out as her release began to ricochet up from the touch of his hands and his cock until she wasn't sure where her flesh ended and his began. Spasms rocked her and she gave in to all of it, caring

nothing for control and giving nothing to hold back.

Chapter Nine

Her climax was so complete that it was long seconds before she
realized that he was simply holding her up, keeping her afloat and
waiting for her to return to reason.

His cock was still rock hard inside of her and an
unmistakable sign that she'd raced ahead. Her eyes fluttered open
and a new anxiety overtook her.

*Oh, god. I'm not sure I can survive that again…not…so*
*soon…*

"Phillip. Don't move. I…need a moment."

He laughed softly and shook his head. "Oh, how familiar
are those words?"

"D-did I not sweetly agree and sit still?"

He withdrew a few inches and drove into her. "Not even
close."

She surrendered to it, a soft inescapable cascade as every thrust of his body changed her equilibrium until it was all she could do to close her eyes, arch her back and ride each wave of wanton heat that rewarded her with another and another. Water sloshed around them both, but they paid no attention outside of the grip of her body and the press of his need.

Phillip's hips jerked with a spasm as his release came, and Serena cried out as she helplessly followed suit, echoing his climax as the heat of his crème flooded her sensitive core. She arched her back and tasted pure feminine power to draw his essence into her body and know that he was hers to rule.

It was like coming home.

Slowly, they disengaged to kneel facing each other in the bath. Their breath was audibly rough from the exercise but neither was so winded that they couldn't laugh from the after effects of passion.

"I'm not sure why I ever…thought…it was possible to converse with a woman in a bathtub." Phillip shook his head, as if to clear it, then his brow furrowed. "Is that…is there scented oil in this water?"

"Jasmine. Like it?"

He smiled with a defeated chuckle. "Let's hope my valet is discreet enough not to ask."

"Phillip. You have to go." She playfully splashed water at him to soften the dismissal. "Pepper will be back at any moment."

"Understood." He stood from the water, treating to her to a breathtaking vision of masculine beauty as rivulets of water slid down his body. Even sated, the size of his manhood made her channel clench in appreciation and hunger. There was a raw primal appeal to every texture and line of him, and Serena openly surveyed him with delight. She loved the dark trail of the hair on his chest the narrow shape of his hips, the broad planes of his chest and carved muscular shift of his thighs as he stepped out of the bath. There was not an inch of him that did not add to a blooming heat inside of her and Serena forced her fingers to grip the tub a little tighter to keep from reaching for him again.

He used the towel and dried off to dress as best he could. Damp clothes clung to his frame and he shook his head slowly. "We may have gotten more water out of the bath than we kept in, Lady Wellcott."

She shrugged. "I'll tell Pepper I slipped and may have splashed a bit."

"A bit?" He gave her a wry grin. "I think I see water drops on the windows over there."

"Are you attempting to convince me not to do this again, Sir Warrick?"

He gathered his boots and stockings up and straightened his shoulders, composing his features into an expression worthy of a butler. "Not at all, madam. I shall leave you to your…bath and see you at dinner, Lady Wellcott."

"Yes. Until tonight. As punishing vengeance goes, Sir Warrick, I'd say this episode is unfolding very nicely."

He smiled and retreated, unlocking the door and surveying the hallway before slipping out.

Serena began to giggle and deliberately slid under the water's surface to keep him from hearing her. The bath had cooled but not enough to temper the fever rebuilding inside of her. She stood to retrieve her towel and climbed out as carefully as she could, wincing at the tender ache between her thighs.

The war between love and hate had become an epic expressed in passion. God how she had craved this! Her pride had yielded to the demands of her body although Serena eyed her reflection with a wary study as she sat at her vanity.

Could she enjoy him without risking her heart? Could she hold herself away from the tangle of her emotions and simply take what pleasure he offered her?

Was that a kind of revenge in and of itself? To prove to him that he was nothing more than a passing distraction to wile away the quiet of the country?

She narrowed her eyes and leaned into the mirror.

*You're playing with fire, Raven Wells.*

She pushed back with a wicked defiant smile. It had been seven years since she'd felt the blaze of his touch and the subject did not bear up under mental study. She picked up a hair brush to smooth out her curls.

*What difference does it make? Am I not a free woman to take what pleasures I can? And if Phillip Warrick is tamed and brought to heel in the process, then who am I to complain?*

Pepper sat at the long table downstairs in the servants dining hall. As with many houses, this room was the hub of all gossip and news for the family above. The servants were the engine that was never seen but without their labors, life above stairs would grind to a miserable halt. Pepper liked the pride in their eyes for the beauty of the house, and listened carefully as their conversations skirted around Mr. Osborne in all things. The housekeeper reminded them of Mrs. Osborne's flower club meetings in the village or chided the cook to be sure to include Mrs. Osborne's favorite dessert after Dell revealed that her lady was melancholy.

"I'm to trouble you for small snippets of fabric from Lady Wellcott's gowns," Dell said softly. "My mistress desires to copy her fashions as closely as possible."

Pepper smiled. "Lady Wellcott has asked me to do one better. I am to sketch out the patterns, if you wish."

"Oh! How generous!"

"Easy enough," Pepper said. "I am no great seamstress but I can lay out a pattern from one viewing of a gown."

"It is a talent I envy," Dell sighed.

"I made some butter cakes," Mrs. Byrd, the cook, interrupted as she set a large platter of warm cakes onto the table. "Megan set them too far back in the oven and so the edges are too dark to take upstairs but still tasty."

Megan was a kitchen maid and her cheeks blazed pink. "Sorry, Mrs. Byrd."

"There, there! We all have a day." Mrs. Byrd sighed.

The housekeeper, Mrs. Watson, joined them. "Be sure to leave one or two for Mr. Clayborne or there'll be hell to pay! I've never known a man to favor butter cakes like our Mr. Clayborne."

The butler was the general they respected but also the man they fondly watched over. The under butler was a man named Baker who clearly carried the weight that an aging Mr. Clayborne no longer could. The transition would inevitably come but from what Pepper could see, Mr. Baker was not pushing to seize the helm. They were a rare coalition marred only by the actions of their master.

Dell shyly took a butter cake and Pepper followed suit. The cakes were delicious and Pepper wondered if the cook hadn't used some flimsy excuse to share with the hardworking staff.

None of the little bites looked burnt to her eyes and the smiles across the table over the treat confirmed it.

"What do you have there, Miss Pepper?" one of the maid's asked.

Pepper held up one of the pretty heeled shoes from her lap. "I'm sewing new bows on my lady's shoes. One was lost and I am taking this chance while she bathes to ensure that they match her newest gown for tonight."

"Shall I send up maids with more hot water, Miss Wellcott?" the housekeeper asked addressing her by her mistress' name as was the custom.

Pepper shook her head. "There's no need. It was scalding to start and I know better. My mistress prefers her privacy and will not thank me for the attention."

The housekeeper nodded her approval. "A good lady's maid is always attuned to her mistress. The best never need to hear the bell before they are on their feet."

The cook laughed. "You say these things so solemnly I almost believe them, Mrs. Watson!"

The banter came in easy rounds until the bows were fixed and Pepper started to rise to take the shoes back up.

"Oh, please wait!" Dell urged her.

"Yes, pardon Miss Wellcott. But…wait until your mistress rings for you or let one of us walk up with you." Sally chimed in.

Dell lowered her voice. "Daws is up to help Mr. Osborne change. Wait until the master's come down, then you can go."

Pepper kept her seat. "As you say."

"The footmen are nearly done setting out the dinner service and one of them can walk you up as well," Megan said.

"Seems a lot of trouble just to carry up a pair of shoes," Pepper said, aware of all the subtle looks around the room. "May I have a word with you privately, Mrs. Watson?"

"Of course." She guided Pepper to her small office next to the storage room and Pepper passed her the small elegant note that Lady Wellcott had prepared. "This. My lady asks you to read it and do what you can. It would serve Mrs. Osborne but also every woman in this house, Mrs. Watson. You need not answer today, but if you agree, please let me know by some word."

Mrs. Watson took the folded paper, openly curious and intrigued. "I shall read it eagerly to see what it says."

Pepper curtsied and began to retreat as the bell in Lady Wellcott's bedroom jangled on the board. "I should attend my lady. If you'll excuse me."

Mrs. Watson nodded her assent and Pepper hurried up the stairs, confident that everyone below stairs would gladly play their part in whatever the game required in the days ahead.

She reached the safety of Serena's bedroom with relief and quickly set about her duties. But something in the way her lady was already sitting at the vanity and brushing out her hair, the ruin of the bedding and signs that when she'd exited the bath, Serena had made no effort to spare the floors—all of it caught Pepper's attention. Water had sloshed everywhere and Pepper knelt to recover the carpets and wooden polished planks then leaned back on her ankles to study her mistress.

"What?"

Pepper's gaze narrowed. "You look rather prim over there, Lady Wellcott."

"Do I?" Serena answered without looking at her. "The bath was very…refreshing."

Pepper stood with a smile, all the pieces falling into place. "Oh, yes! Nothing restores a woman like a long, hot, delicious…soak."

Serena turned on her chair quickly, her eyes sparkling. "Pepper!"

"I've got the gold all pressed and I'll hang it here, on the screen, my lady." Pepper was all business, merrily preparing for the next change. It was her secret belief that no matter what her friend said, she had never let go of her affection for Sir Warrick. "My goodness! I'd better see to this. We wouldn't want anyone to think you'd been wrestling alligators this afternoon."

"Pepper."

Pepper finished drying the floor and then danced to press her weight against the towel to tamp up what moisture she could from the carpets, then risked a playful glance at Serena. "Oh, did you wish to take a nap? Perhaps to rest after the rigors of washing?"

"Oh, stop it, Prudence!" Serena blushed. "You are not nearly as clever as you think you are."

Pepper said little but began to help her dress, making note of the subtle marks on Serena's body that betrayed all. Serena's entire visage was calmer and even younger, as if she'd tasted an elixir that had lightened her spirit.

Pepper took the brush from the table and began to braid and tame Serena's black tresses, adding the gold combs with a skilled hand.

*I'm clever enough to know when you're happy, Raven Wells.*

Chapter Ten

The gold dress was one of her favorites because of the way it shimmered in the candlelight. Its daring cut was more suited to a grand ball than a quiet country dinner but she didn't care. She wanted to feel her power, to draw on that well of confidence within her like a shield. She felt more vulnerable than she had in a long time but also more alive. As Phillip sat across from her, her body was still tingling from their lovemaking, Serena prayed that he couldn't read her.

"Did you have a good ride, cousin?" Delilah asked him innocently.

"What?" Phillip stiffened in his seat, his cheeks reddening before he realized his mistake. "Oh, yes...I went out for a ride. It was very brisk."

"Good exercise, I'm sure," James added as he helped himself to a fish fillet from the platter that Mr. Clayborne held out for him. "Wish I'd gotten out to join you. God, I am confined like a monk!"

Delilah's eyes dropped to her plate and Serena did her best to intervene. "The demands of your business kept you indoors, did they? How taxing! I always imagine it is hard for men to be restricted so! Your energies must demand action, do they not?"

She'd meant to aim the barb at James but it was Phillip's smoldering look that nearly robbed her of speech. *God, this is like juggling on a tightrope!*

"It is unnatural for a man to be trapped with a room full of ledgers!" James sighed, then glanced at Phillip. "Not that I might not have accepted an invitation to slip away if one had been extended to me."

Phillip smiled. "The ride wasn't planned. Perhaps next time I leave the house for exercise, I'll include you, James."

"Tomorrow, then!" James announced. "The weather promises to be fine and I am not going to be left behind, sir!"

"Very well," Phillip conceded smoothly. "Though if you pout like a four year old, I may be tempted to slip out the back door to avoid you, cousin."

James laughed. "As if you would dare!"

"There is very little I will not dare," Phillip countered, his gaze shifting to Serena in her gold gown. "Would the ladies care to join us?"

Serena shook her head. "We will leave you to it. I shall keep my dear Mrs. Osborne company tomorrow. I have neglected her too much recently."

Delilah smiled. "You are very kind."

"She is very kind. Why is she not married?" James asked without preamble.

"James!" Delilah gasped.

"What? Lady Wellcott is your dear friend and can we not ask a simple question without you huffing and puffing like a hysteric over there, wife!" James tapped his glass for more wine and looked at Serena. "You are too young to play the matron, Lady Wellcott. Don't you think?"

She took a sip of her own wine before she replied. "I am not married because I do not wish to be."

James' brow furrowed in confusion. "What woman doesn't wish to be married?"

"This woman." Serena wasn't in the mood to give the man any quarter. "Did you misunderstand me, Mr. Osborne? I was so proud of myself for speaking plainly."

James' confusion didn't relent. "Phillip! Here is your chance to jump in and make a case for all the lovely delights that marriage can bring!"

Serena laughed. "How amusing that a married man would defer to a bachelor to make his point!"

Phillip shook his head, smiling. "I was about to say the same thing."

"A woman in your position must surely be seeking to find a good match!" James persisted. "Is it not the natural way of things?"

"Leave off it," Phillip's humor faded. "Lady Wellcott is your guest, James, and I'm fairly certain that badgering her about such personal matters is not in good taste."

"It is in the worst taste, James," Delilah said with a firm quiet. "What has gotten into you this evening?"

James scowled at her. "God! Since when did a question of practical matters become so unspeakable in decent company?" He stood abruptly and threw down his napkin. "Forgive me then. I'll be in my study for brandy and cigars."

He began to leave the room then hesitated at the door. "Phillip?"

Phillip didn't move except to cut his fish. "I'm still eating."

"Where is your loyalty?" James demanded.

"With my stomach and the dulcet presence of the ladies over your bellowing about your hurt feelings, cousin. But I will join you in a while if that appeases."

"You're a traitor." James closed the door behind him and they all began to smile, like guilty children who had driven off an irrational tutor.

"I apologize. James is…out of sorts," Delilah began.

"No need to apologize, Mrs. Osborne." Serena said graciously.

*James' deteriorating mood was a good sign that he wasn't faring well during his involuntary celibacy. Just as I'd predicted...*

"I—I should—go check on—" Delilah suddenly stood as well, the color draining from her face. "I don't feel well."

Phillip stood reflexively and Serena realized that it was fear on Delilah's face.

*Dell.*

*She is going to make sure that Dell is out of reach!*

"Of course. Sir Warrick and I can entertain ourselves until you return." Serena assured her before Delilah raced from the room without another word.

"My god! Is she…going to be all right?" Phillip said.

"Undoubtedly."

He sat down slowly. "This has been a dinner I won't soon forget."

"A fitting end for the day?"

"I can think of better ways I would hope to end this day."

"Can you, Sir Warrick?" Serena sighed flirtatiously, savoring the way he was looking at her, the way his gaze warmed her skin.

The rest of the meal transformed into a quiet playful duel as they each purposefully followed the strict rules and polite forms of conduct. With the footmen in the room, they deliberately kept the conversation to general topics; the weather, mutual acquaintances, impressions of Southgate Hall and its views.

They lingered over a final glass of wine and then bid each other a polite, courteous good night.

"Good night, Sir Warrick." She stood and he immediately did the same.

"Lady Wellcott."

It was a glorious little game where they climbed the stairs, Serena ten risers ahead of him completely aware of his steps behind her. Not another word was spoken as they each went to their respective bedrooms, readied for bed, dismissed their attendants and counted the seconds before she knocked on his door to gain admittance.

"Lady Wellcott," he said softly. "What a delightful surprise."

"Is it?" She rewarded him with a wicked smile that instantly clouded his intellect. "I wonder what you will say at my next effort to shock you."

"No doubt," he said as cavalierly as he could as his body began to tighten, "it will be something completely eloquent and—"

She slipped the lace edged robe back from her shoulders to let it fall at her feet, revealing that she wore nothing beneath. Her black hair was a cascade of silk down her back with several long tendrils that lay over her shoulder to draw his eyes down across her body, her breasts and the triangle of dark curls between her hips. She smelled faintly of jasmine scented water, the perfumed oil in her hair and the musk of sexual arousal.

Everything about her was an open invitation to his senses.

"What say you now, Sir Warrick?"

He wasn't saying anything. He pulled her against him, kissing her in a thorough assault that had nothing to do with polite speeches or a slow, reserved approach to taking what he needed. Because God help him, whatever tame or measured thread of "want" he'd held onto was lost in a blaze of raw need. He needed her, as he needed to breathe. There was no question, no choice, no option left but this woman in his arms.

It made no sense but his life was worthless without the contact of her skin against his. He hated the gnawing realization that if he'd meant to "win her", he'd been a fool. For there was only surrender to be had and he didn't care.

She boldly reached out to caress him through the soft cloth of his pants. "What does it feel like, Phillip? To grow hard?"

"It feels…like fine hot sand sliding down my spine. It feels heavy and gloriously tight as if I'm stretching a muscle but without effort. No…no effort at all," he sighed and shifted his hips forward to fill her hands and prolong her touch against his sensitive shaft.

She lifted her face to beg him for more kisses and any interest in education was abandoned. He bent over to lift her from the floor and carry her to his bed, kissing her all the while and sampling the siren in his arms.

He lay her down in the center of the great feather bed then shed his robe and pants to climb up onto the mattress. Phillip sat back on his heels and took in the beauty of Serena sprawled across his bed. Her breasts were firm and high, the dark points proudly jutting up toward the ceiling; her nipples already pebble hard with desire. Her thighs had fallen apart and she made no effort to hide her silky damp sex from him. She was a confection of wanton display and his eyes lingered to savor every detail.

"Phillip," she said with a pout. "When a naked woman presents herself, it is not solely for study."

He smiled. "Truly? Well, then. Let me see if I can remedy my lady's impatient state."

"I did *not* say I was impatient if—" Serena gasped. "Oh!"

He lifted her foot to plant a kiss on her instep, and then began to work his way upward effectively ending her planned speech. It was a leisurely assault that lingered on the sensitive concave hollows behind her knees and then feasted on the pillow-soft curves of her inner thighs. The scent of her body grew and he watched as clear honey coated her folds and betrayed his success.

He teased her, kissing the curls above her sex until she began to shake and writhe in frustration. He was as eager as she for the moment and finally yielded to his own need to taste her. He dipped his tongue into the red silk of her body and almost cried out in joy at the sweet flavor of her arousal against his mouth. He stilled her with his fingers firmly splayed against her hips to hold her in place and settled in to the quest to drink her release.

Every pass of his tongue over her clit made her buck and cry out, so Phillip slowed down the game, teasing her lips, kissing and suckling her until she was so ready he feared he'd held off too long. Feather light flicks of his tongue met the taut little pearl, steady and insistent, until the rhythm of his mouth against her sensitive nub caught up to her desires and overtook her senses completely. He mastered her with the barest contact, working her flesh until she was enslaved to it, until every nerve ending in her body was thrumming with the connection to this tiny place and the slick caresses of his tongue.

She came in a beautiful trembling cascade that he drank in, refusing to slow down or yield until he had had his fill of the intoxicating musk of her body. He lifted his mouth only to slip one of his fingers inside of the molten channel, gasping as her muscles tightened and gripped him, pushing into her release and extending the pleasure until she had to cover her own mouth to keep from screaming with it.

*You are mine, Serena.*

*You are mine, Raven.*

*You are mine, woman.*

He relented and withdrew his hand but kissed her gently as he did. He raised himself up on his elbows to assess how she was faring. Serena raised herself up on her elbows as well, blinking as if she had just woken up. Her color was high, staining her cheeks pink and she gifted him with an astonished smile.

"That was…lovely."

"Was it?" he asked softly. "Well, let us see how we can improve the experience."

"What?" Her eyes widened. "I don't—think improvements are necessary!"

He replied silently by continuing the explorations he'd begun from her feet, bending over to kiss the rise of her belly, trailing his tongue around the miniature well of her belly button. He kissed it reverently before moving on to nip at the lines of her waist and then her ribs, tracing each one until she was once again a writhing siren beneath him.

He slowly admired every inch, every change that time had wrought, ignoring the impatient demands of his own body.

Now there was only Serena.

And his determination to take the slow road.

"I read once that some women can climax just from a man's attention to their breasts."

"How…brazen of them!"

"Hmm." He eyed her breasts like a man contemplating a new approach to paradise.

"Phillip!" Serena covered her breasts defensively with her hands. "I see no need to prove every sexual theory that comes into your head."

He smiled. "No? I am surprised at you, Lady Wellcott. Where is your adventurous spirit? Unless of course, you've shriveled up into some kind of prim version of—"

She punched him in the shoulder. "Quiet yourself, Warrick, or I'll show you what a woman pushed to adventure is capable of!"

"God, yes!" he sighed. He kissed her so that she could taste herself on his lips, his hands replacing hers to cover her breasts, mapping her body to claim once and for all. His thigh slid between hers and he deliberately shifted up until her wet folds were riding the ridge of his upper leg. He kissed her deeper, the friction of his hand against her nipples and against her slick soft flesh, played out in a concert of worship and sensation.

She came again, this time in a ragged primal dance that inspired him to push her even further. He parted her thighs easily, lining up his body before she was aware of him, and buried himself inside of her, gritting his teeth to fight a quick finish. He moved only enough to draw out her release, only enough to change the rhythm of her body's demands, slowing the waves only to build them one on top of another until she was mindless with it.

She bit his shoulder and he smiled at the pain as she inadvertently helped him to maintain control. *My poor darling!*

He relented slightly, easing up on the pace to let her catch her breath, but Phillip wasn't about to stop. They'd both waited too long to be cheated.

She caressed his back with her hands then shifted them to trail over his chest, gently pinching his nipples and playfully exploring his body even as he continued to drive slowly inside of her.

She eyed with a sly smile. "You were skinnier then, sir."

He groaned and rolled his eyes. "God, you know how to flatter a man, Lady Wellcott!"

"You weren't as muscular and fit then and—Phillip Warrick! You know very well that you have a very handsome physique and are a breathtaking example of male prowess! There. Does that soothe?"

His cock hardened even more at the compliments despite his intent to pretend he was unmoved and try to get her to keep going. Apparently hearing Serena praise his body was no small pleasure without impact. Her smile evaporated with a gasp as the change in his physique registered on her own.

"Did you want to say anything else, Serena?"

"You mean, besides making the gentle observation that you mysteriously smell like jasmine bath oil? A very intriguing change, do you not agree?"

"Oh, you'll pay for that jest, woman."

He withdrew quickly and flipped her over onto her belly. She squeaked in mild protest as he pushed a pillow under her hips to raise them for his pleasure. Phillip allowed himself a second or two to admire the view of her bottom in the air like a ripe peach with the inviting seam of her sex; but a second or two was all he allowed.

"Phillip!"

He notched the plum-sized head of his cock against her, closing his eyes at the shiver of lust that seized him as her molten flesh stretched to encase him. He knew she was almost too sensitive for more, but Phillip couldn't show her mercy.

She was teetering on the edge. Phillip took one deep breath and plunged ahead, pushing them both on until there was nothing in their way. He came into her slowly, with small measured thrusts that gave her no time to settle before he withdrew and then pressed a little deeper. She writhed at the sweet torment until he was finally buried inside of her completely. She wriggled her hips and lifted them higher only to cry out at the tight spasm of pleasure that seized her when the searing hot head of his cock came in contact with her inner core and a surprising hidden trigger that promised nothing but ecstasy. Serena's eyes widened at shock. She'd long considered herself a woman entirely aware of her own anatomy but here was something new.

But apparently not an unknown thing to her lover.

Phillip moved quickly to take advantage of her reaction, unable to hold back any longer. The coil of tension between his hip bones exploded in an orgasm that robbed him of breath. He climaxed in a jet of a white hot release that ripped a primal growl from his throat. Phillip shuddered at the waves, marveling that intensity of his pleasure bordered on pain.

*Damn it. If I come to my senses and realize I'm crying, I swear I won't be surprised...*

Thankfully, he wasn't unmanned with tears, but it was several long minutes before he could remember how to talk.

"Holy...dear god...that was..." Phillip struggled to catch his breath.

"Phillip?" she said softly, as they gently disengaged to collapse in each other's arms.

"Yes?"

"I am becoming convinced that...slow is...a feast I shall have to grow accustomed to..." She kissed his shoulder. "I shall never tease you about rushing again."

"Ah, then it was worth it!" he said with a proud smile. "Although, we can make a rushed attempt if you need to make another objective comparison. Just...give me a few minutes to recover."

She sat up in astonishment drawing the sheet up around her. "You cannot be serious!"

"You are as addictive as opium, Lady Wellcott. But, alas…no. I may need more than a few minutes before I can forever impress you with my prowess and staying powers."

She laughed. "Thank God!" She was quiet for a few seconds and then looked at him flirtatiously through the veil of her lashes. "I'd forgotten how transformative the act is. It is a wonder that anyone bothers to do anything else!"

He shook his head with a smile. "What a wicked thing you are!"

"To your benefit apparently." She tipped her head to one side. "Is it not strange that you say it like a compliment when I am naked but as an insult when I have my clothes on?"

"You mystify, Lady Wellcott. One moment I think I know you, then the next…"

"Blame my upbringing. Lord Trent civilized me just enough, didn't he? He refined my manners so that I could blend into any good salon or charm at the dinner table but not so much that I wouldn't remain a wild creature inside. I was hungry for affection and pleasure and he never dissuaded me. There were no moral lessons in my schoolroom and no boundaries between my desires and my actions."

He shook his head. "You—were not unaware of right and wrong, Serena."

She laughed. "Perhaps. I was a child then. Trent made sure I was ripe for the taking and I still marvel at fate. For if not you, it could have been any man if Trent had been diverted from his path, his hunger for vengeance. I wanted love like a flower craves the sun. Trent saw to all of it. He put me in your path. He'd trained me like an animal to never say no to a man's wishes and my own whims and impulses were fuel to the fire." She shrugged her pale shoulders. "I was a virgin but I was far from innocent. I was like a feral creature in the guise of a porcelain doll and I'm wise enough to see how appealing that is to a man."

A shiver tripped down his spine. "Not just a simple twist of fate, Serena. Not just any man. Me. You were meant for me and I don't care how casually you wish to belittle it. This fire between us is far more than the work of fate's clock."

She touched his face, cooling the heat of anger there but also subtly reigniting the embers of his desire. "You are right. It could not have been any man. I don't think even in Trent's wildest dreams he accounted for how completely I would fall for you or how it would change me."

She stood and turned, retrieving her robe from the floor to shake it out and pull it back on. She tied the sash firmly around her waist and raked her fingers through her hair to magically tame it back into a single twist that fell down her back. "There, I am restored."

"Stay."

She shook her head. "I dare not. For whatever would the servants think, sir? I am a respected woman and must do all I can to protect my good name." Her smile was bewitching as she resumed the illusions of social order. "As you must recall that you are a guest in your cousin's home and bound to not dishonor your family with scandal."

He sighed. "What would it be like to love you openly? How is it that I am always trapped in a strange web of deception when it comes to you? If James is eager to play the matchmaker and Delilah is a dear friend and sure to approve, why are we lurking about in darkened hallways again?"

The playfulness in her eyes evaporated. "If you wish to earn my trust and affection, you will do as I bid. You may be ready to play out some public show of..." Her lip curled in disgust. "I am not so inclined. I am not ready to risk humiliation and destruction at your hands, Sir Warrick. You and I are not..." She crossed her arms defensively. "The risk would once again be entirely mine. You think a tumble or two means that I am at your feet, sir? I may crave you but that is a condition you can either continue to enjoy, or we can end it now."

He raised his hands in a gesture of surrender. "Whoa! No need to hiss and spit! I will keep your secrets for as long as you wish. Though truthfully, I intend to outlast your fears, Lady Wellcott. I will prove that the last things I would ever bring to you are humiliation or destruction. There will be no repetition of the mistakes of the past, Serena. How could there be?"

She pressed her lips together into a tight line of unhappiness, her eyes clouding with wary distrust and frustration.

"How? How could there be?" She sighed. "We'll see, won't we?"

She slipped out the door and shut it behind her before he could think of an answer to soothe the storm in her eyes.

*She wants me but she doesn't trust me.*

He couldn't blame her for it. His own wounds were troublesome enough but they surely paled in comparison to all that she had suffered. Phillip couldn't retrace his steps. All he could do was pray that there was still a path ahead to let him prove to her that the future they'd lost was still within reach.

In the meantime, he would close his eyes and try to enjoy the dictations of Lady Serena Wellcott as she engineered a dizzying game of sexual cat and mouse in a physical contest of catch and release. For Phillip, he accepted that he would dare anything to achieve her. No woman had stirred his heart since the nightmare of Trent's making and he was hungry to finally repair his life and move forward.

*I'll hold steady and she'll abandon her need for secrecy.*

*In time, she'll see that secrets serve neither of us in the end.*

Serena made it to her room before her composure began to crumble. She stumbled with a surprised cry into a small table by the door and swallowed the bitter bile that rose in her throat. Every bittersweet exchange with him was costing her too much. Serena had put her heel on the neck of more men than she could call to memory, but Phillip eluded her control. Worse, he brought back memories she'd long banished and provoked her raw emotions to such an extent she was sure to say too much and stumble against him.

To stumble against him and never let go.

He sought to heal the rift between them unaware of how wide the chasm stood. Whatever part of her hungered for him, needed him, there was a deadly streak of awareness that there would never be a happy ending for the woman that she had become.

Serena took in a few slow breaths and waited for her heart to accept what her mind knew as true. She waited until the echoes of pleasure inside of her faded and there was nothing left but the beating of her own heart.

*Whatever it is between us, it is fleeting.*

*It is a simple distraction that will have to be managed.*

*And when my business with Mrs. Osborne is finished, it will*

*end.*

*Once and for all.*

Chapter Eleven

"Did you find Dell last night?" Serena asked and began to pour the tea.

"Yes. It was a—foolish impulse to bolt like that but James was so..." Delilah let out a shaky breath. "I suddenly couldn't breathe and the thought that instead of going to the library he might have gone upstairs to ring the bell in my bedroom. She'd have answered it believing it to be me and..."

"Is that how he tricked her when it happened?"

"Yes. Just that easily."

Serena held out a teacup. "Here. To settle your nerves." Delilah took it and Serena stirred her own. "I said nothing but your claim to be unwell will only provide more credence to what you've told James. That is, *if* it is reported to him that you left the table abruptly last night."

"I've done as you asked, Lady Wellcott. I've…hinted to James that I suspect I may be pregnant at last." Delilah fanned herself slowly. "He was not as joyously cheered as I'd hoped but he has been sleeping in his dressing room."

Serena smiled. "And taking his sour mood out on Sir Warrick."

"I think he is quite fond of you, Lady Wellcott. Truly and genuinely fond."

"Hardly but I think Sir Warrick and I have reached a détente." Serena sighed. "But back to James. If he has shifted his sleeping arrangements, then he is giving credence to your claim."

"For a time," Delilah said. "But what will I do when he discovers my deception?"

Serena nodded. "What deception? There *is* a baby coming, is there not, Mrs. Osborne?"

Delilah quietly worked through the implications of it all and Serena marveled at how beautiful her expression became when the revelation settled against her heart. "Oh, yes! Yes, there is!"

"I think it might be a fitting addition to our scheme if your husband's child could be acknowledged as such and if you can summon the generosity it would require to give it your family's name…" Serena knew that there was no debate to be had but it was important that Delilah see all the pieces fall into place.

"Dell! What a relief to my Dell! If together we could raise this child!" Delilah pressed her hands against her chest. "It would be more than fitting. It would be a blessing I cannot give credence!"

"Depending on how things play out in the next week, we will protect the child at all costs. Sit with this for a time, Mrs. Osborne. As you love Dell, I think you can love this baby and steal the future away from James. For you are now the architect of the years to come, not your husband, and if you have room for his baby, then I think it will be a very beautiful life ahead."

"But James would never allow—"

"James will have no say in the matter. None. And if he is wise, he'll simply be grateful to see his family name carried on and his line continue." Serena shrugged her shoulders. "Or I'll make sure he is."

"What a tangle! However do you keep all the threads set in your mind, Lady Wellcott?" Delilah took a sip of her tea. "You are a marvel to me!"

"I do what I must. It isn't much of a parlor trick at the end of the day."

"Do you mind if I ask…"

"You may ask me anything, Mrs. Osborne."

"What is the worst revenge you have ever meted out, Lady Wellcott?"

"Why do you ask that question?"

"I think I want to take courage but also to brace myself for whatever is to come."

Serena smiled. "Wise. Very well, but please keep in mind that every plan unfolds differently and no one's revenge is a match to another's."

"Understood."

"There once was a Lord L, let us call him. His wife reached out to the Black Rose and it was a meeting I have never forgotten. For her husband's cruelty was so horrifying and so all encompassing, it stole my breath."

"Did he...beat her?" Delilah asked softly, her eyes already wide.

Serena nodded. "No but his cruelty had no bounds. His every word to her was barbed, his every action aimed at hurting her, frightening her, and tormenting her. Even so, she'd have dutifully endured if he hadn't finally gone too far for her soul to absorb." Serena sighed. "She had a little dog, a black-faced pug who was her dear companion and her one solace in this world."

"Oh, god! Please...say no more."

"He drowned it in front of her," Serena finished mercilessly.

Delilah's eyes filled with tears. "No!"

"Needless to say, upon hearing her tale, I was more than happy to take the commission."

"What did you do?" Delilah whispered.

Serena smiled at the delicious memory. "Poor Lord L! Weeks of planning but there was a grand masque ball that provided just the opportunity I needed. A small touch of seduction on my part to lead him upstairs and a few drops of a potent drug in his glass..."

"Yes?" Delilah asked, on the edge of her seat.

"He awoke to a nursemaid's screams quickly followed by the lady of the house and several guests."

"Did they find you abed together?"

Serena shook her head and laughed. "Oh, no! For a man such as that, a small indiscretion like infidelity would hardly matter! I conjured a sin he could never laugh away. Lord L was found in a most compromising position with his pants around his aristocratic ankles in the nursery of his host's six year old son."

"No!" Delilah's astonishment and horror was total. "How could you? That poor innocent child!"

"I may be a heartless villain but I have my principles!" Serena's mirth faded fast. "I would *never* harm a child! The boy was fast asleep and oblivious to all after a few drops of laudanum were put into his bedtime's sweet milk. Lord L *never* touched that child!" She smoothed out her skirts. "I had the help of a few paid insiders to arrange all and ensure that the boy would be unscathed. They even tucked the small bottle of laudanum in Lord L's waistcoat pocket for good measure. It was a thoughtful detail to add to the scene and so impossible for Lord L to explain."

"What if the child had awoken?"

Serena shook her head. "Trust me. He awoke the next morning like a cherub in his own nursery and reportedly had a dream about dancing bears. You are concentrating on the wrong elements, Mrs. Osborne." Serena reached over to take her hand. "Here, let's try this again, Delilah! Picture it. Lord L ensnared in what could only be viewed as an act of attempted rape and buggery with a helpless child under his host's roof and over the heads of every influential member of the nobility you can fit into a grand house at the height of the social season! It was a masterpiece!"

"Oh, my!" Delilah's cheeks colored and her eyes sparkled. "It's terrible but...so wonderful at the same time, isn't it?"

Serena nodded. "There, now you have the way of it! I was in the ballroom in the midst of a waltz when the excitement unfolded so I can tell you with utter certainty that word of the crime had spread like wildfire before the music of my dance had ended."

"So quickly!" Delilah exclaimed.

"It was ruin, total and complete."

"And Lady L?"

"She would have petitioned for a divorce and achieved her freedom without a blink of protest." Serena folded her hands together. "She would have, but that was the one wrinkle in the plan I had not foreseen."

"She did not? How could she not divorce him after all of that?"

"There was no need." Serena reached up to tuck a black curl back into place atop her head. "He hung himself the next day."

"Oh," Delilah was at a loss for words.

Serena shrugged her shoulders. "A tidier end than he deserved, Mrs. Osborne, though he did give his wife one final ironic comforting gift on his way to Hades."

"And what gift was that?"

"He used her dog's leash to end himself." Serena sighed. "I like to think that some part of him knew the true source of his downfall."

"What a tale!" Delilah pressed her fingers to her temples. "Was Lady L…happy? After it was over?"

"Deliriously." Serena nodded and poured herself another cup of tea. "I sent her a basket of pug puppies wearing bright yellow ribbons after the funeral. We correspond regularly and her letters are a source of delight to me. She is a strong and vibrant member of our little society, Mrs. Osborne."

Delilah's expression dimmed.

"What troubles you?" Serena asked.

"I must be a wretched person, Lady Wellcott. For just then—I felt nothing but envy. Envy for a widow because she is free, so completely free, isn't she?"

Serena reached across to take Delilah's hand. "Every path is different. My plans do not set out to make you a widow, Mrs. Osborne. But I don't think you will be disappointed in the justice we achieve. I promise."

Delilah nodded. "I trust you completely."

"How is your Dell?"

"Fearful but not for herself. She is convinced that my husband will take his revenge on me if he learns of my…efforts to move against him."

"Then I should ask how you are faring, Mrs. Osborne."

"Well enough. I feared my resolve would flag but it is the opposite. When I see that look in his eyes, knowing what I do now… I am ashamed that I was so blind to it before and to the pain he inflicted on so many." Delilah's eyes filled with tears. "If you cannot stop him, Lady Wellcott, I do not think I can face it."

"There, there." Serena touched her friend's shoulder. "The Black Rose has you in hand and he will be stopped. It won't be long and then we shall never speak of shame again. Never."

Delilah nodded slowly, her composure recovering slowly. "Thank you, Lady Wellcott."

"After." Serena sat back and took a genteel sip from her teacup. "Thank me after."

Chapter Twelve

That night, Serena carefully crept downstairs in stocking feet. Her confident assurances to Delilah had spurred her into action. It was just after midnight and the entire house was settled into a deep slumber, though she suspected Phillip would be awaiting her upstairs. The hem of her velvet wrap whispered over the carpets and floors behind her and she navigated with the tips of her fingers along the balustrade and wood paneling in the main hall. She approached the door to James study with caution, expecting to find it locked. But the heavy carved door gave way at a light touch to reveal Mr. Osborne's masculine sanctuary.

A full moon provided ample light through the large ground floor windows behind the desk. She'd counted on it and not bothered fumbling with a candle and risking discovery. Serena moved into the room and took a seat behind the desk. The drawers were locked but she overcame them easily with the small toolkit she'd brought with her. The wealthy Lady Wellcott had learned from the best pickpockets and criminals in London's darkest heart. She could cheat at cards, forge any handwriting like a master and shoot a coin set atop a post at twenty-five paces.

She began to look through what papers were there, seeking additional information on her quarry; any surprising avenues to his back, IOU's or evidence of debt, signs of gambling, or financial stress. Serena studied everything, praying that one of his ledgers would give her another advantage. The simple plan that had started to coalesce in her mind was all well and good, but Serena preferred to have more than one weapon at her disposal.

After all, the worst men never fought fairly, so why should she?

But there was nothing.

She forced herself to slow down and make sure that there weren't any hidden drawers before finally abandoning the search. She put everything back as she'd found it and relocked the drawers. Then put her leather bound toolkit into her robe's pocket as she stood up and surveyed the desk again to make sure that nothing was out of place…not even the chair.

She retreated to close the door to the study and begin retracing her steps back up the stairs; a ghost in the hallways moving without sound.

She froze at the sight of another ghost standing outside her bedroom door, then smiled. "Phillip."

"What are you doing out—"

She pressed her fingertips against his lips. "Shh! I was sleepwalking."

"Sleepwalking?" he whispered.

"I dreamt a handsome man was seeking me…"

He smiled and began to guide her through the doorway to her bedroom. "If you spoil this moment and start describing that man as a foreigner with dark hair, I am going to be very disappointed, Lady Wellcott."

She giggled and shut the door firmly behind them, locking it. "How presumptuous of you, Sir Warrick! I can assure you he was a good deal taller than you are and—"

He kissed her to teach her a lesson about provoking his jealousy and she was grateful for his firm schooling. She opened up to him like a flower, eagerly tasting the balm of his attentions and the victory of distracting him from any questions about what she'd been doing downstairs.

And then she was the one distracted beyond questioning.

Chapter Thirteen

The next morning, Raven prepared for the day in the rituals of beauty that Pepper orchestrated. While her curls were arranged, Raven opened her jewelry box on the vanity table and selected an object with deliberate care. "Here."

It was an ornate hair ornament and a favorite that had served her well in the past. The hair pin was nearly six inches in length and almost as thick as a child's littlest finger. Topped with a flat jade carving of a bird, the shaft appeared to be embossed metal with vines and flowers in bas relief but the decorations were merely a grip atop a solid sheath where the true nature of the hair pin nested. Raven touched the carved jade head of the hair pin, pulling it up just an inch to note that the blade inside was still razor sharp. She didn't know the origins of the miniature stiletto after buying it from a small antique shop in London years ago but wearing the strange little weapon gave her courage.

"I'll wear it tonight and then at every occasion forward." Serena held it up against her hair to admire the way her hair provided a dark foil for the jade's magical green. It was a deliberate choice to wear it all the time, so that its appearance would not draw any attention. After a day or two, the addition to her fashion would be no change at all and instead a subtle and familiar detail for no one to note. "See that it is prepared first and then again every morning."

"Truly?"

"You think the request so drastic? My instincts say otherwise. James Osborne is…" Serena's gaze shifted to her own reflection and the calm glittering fury there. "James Osborne is about to fall."

Pepper nodded. "Good enough. There's not a maid below stairs that doesn't wish him a gruesome end."

Serena turned in her chair quickly. "Damn it. Not just Dell then."

"Dell was only the latest from what I could glean. But the housemaids never work the upper floors alone and no scullery maid is sent to clean out the fireplaces or bring up coal without a footman at the ready to come to her aid." Pepper shook out her mistress's night rail. "It's the best proof of it if the house's procedures are set to protect the weakest in the house from their master's attentions."

"Delilah said she suspected that there was more and that she'd taken precautions."

"Mrs. Osborne is beloved for her kindness among the staff. I believe they hid the worst from her out of love, my lady, not to protect their master." Pepper sat on the bed. "If it were me, I'd not spend a night under this roof as a housemaid. The man makes my blood freeze with fear."

"Pepper? Have you had an encounter with Mr. Osborne?"

Pepper shrugged her shoulders. "Just in passing when I was coming up yesterday with your shoes. Remember? The bow had come loose?"

Serena sighed. "Forget the bow. Tell me what happened, please dearest."

"He was coming down the hallway and I stepped to the wall, eyes down, like a good servant should. Never seen to be seen is the rule!" Pepper's cheeks gained a little pink. "He didn't say a word but damned if he didn't slow down and make a point of walking past me so close his legs brushed my skirts. I took a peek and that devil was looking at me like a plate of cakes!"

"My god!"

"I nearly fainted dead away, I will confess," she said. "But he didn't stop and not a word did he offer—and god knows, I was so grateful I never thought to complain about it later."

"Pepper! You should have told me immediately!"

"What! It was only yesterday and I have told you as soon as I could." Pepper cleared her throat, a prim expression stealing over her features. "It's not as if my darling lady has been in her rooms much of late."

A curse slipped past her lips and it was Serena's turn to struggle with a blush. "I have lingered too long over...the question of Sir Warrick. Phillip distracted me from my original purpose here and I—I am embarrassed at the lapse. But I will amend the mistake. Delilah has been patient long enough and time is quickly running out."

Pepper clapped her hands in anticipation. "I do enjoy it when you get that determined spark in your eyes."

"Dell's condition is bound to betray her soon." Serena stood to begin to pace out of habit. "I need to drive him to ground."

"Yes. But how?"

Serena took a deep breath. Risk was part of her life. Every venture of the Black Rose carried intrinsic threats to her fragile existence as Lady Serena Wellcott but she'd embraced the dangers. It was easy to gamble when you didn't care about your own stake in the game but she cared very much about Pepper. From her years at the orphanage, Pepper had been the little sister and faithful mascot she had never forgotten.

*The instant I had the means and my freedom, I retrieved her to be by my side.*

*Even the Black Rose wouldn't be what it is without Pepper. She was the first one to note that without access to a man's servants, I would always be blinded to his true nature.*

"What are you stewing about over there?" Pepper asked.

"I'm stewing over a nightmare. For this time it's not a well appointed lady that draws out the devil in Mr. Osborne and I fear I am not going to be able to change that fact."

"It's maid servants who stir him, that's as certain as sunrise." Pepper nodded. "And I've already caught his eye! I don't see why you're all twisted and torn over there. I can play my part."

Serena crossed her arms, turning back to face Pepper. "This isn't like securing a bit of gossip or acting the messenger below stairs. This is—far more than that and far more dangerous."

"Dell's a dear and there's not a woman within a thousand miles that should suffer what she has. We've been sharing a room and I confess, I've grown terribly fond of her. If I can help you stop him, then why should I not be up for it? Besides," Pepper added confidently, "you'll not let any harm come to me."

Serena shook her head. "I'd cut my own throat first but if we get this wrong…"

"When has the beautiful Lady Serena Wellcott ever gotten anything wrong?" Pepper laughed, then sobered quickly.

"Mistress. Please. You said yourself time was short. I'm telling you as straight as a sparrow. Do your worst."

Serena finally accepted it and returned to her seat at the vanity, drawing it close to Pepper to keep their conversation private and quiet. "Very well. Then here is the plan. We will keep it simple to try to keep you safe."

"Simple is good."

"Two days from now at breakfast, I will make a point of saying that I have left you alone upstairs in my bedroom with an armful of mending."

"Why would I do the mending in your room and not carry it downstairs in the servant's hall?" Pepper asked.

"Because the light is better in my room and I spoil you."

"Ah!" Pepper smiled. "That rings true!"

"If we make it clear that he has the opportunity he longs for, then when he acts on that impulse, we will have him." Serena reached out to cover one of Pepper's hands with hers. "I will come quickly before harm is done but Pepper, there is the chance…
What if I am wrong? What if he catches you when we are not prepared?"

"You will track him like a falcon, mistress. And when you catch him trying to get at my buttons, we'll make such a scene that his world will come down around his ears, right?" Pepper chimed in, faith shining in her eyes. "And Dell will be safe."

*Dell will be safe. Every maid in the house will be safe. An unborn child will be safe.*

*But what about you, Pepper?*

Serena steadied herself with a long slow breath. "And you will be safe. I swear it."

"So two more days then?"

"Yes. Two days gives me time to make sure that Mrs. Osborne is set, and that there is nothing I've omitted. When I go down to breakfast that morning I will set all in motion and then when he makes his move, we will end him." Serena released her friend's hand and stood, taking on the mantle of her title in the set of her shoulders. "Until then you keep well out of his reach. I have business of my own to finish. Make no move to pack but be ready to leave quickly since these are our last days in the house."

"I won't disappoint you." Pepper also stood to smooth out her apron and reset her mob cap. "No fears, mistress. When the time comes, I'll scream like a banshee and crack the plaster."

Serena shuddered, unable to answer. She walked out of the room before she could change her mind or frighten Pepper with the terror that was nibbling at her nerves. *No fears? Until it's done, I will walk around with a basket full of black adders in my arms.*

*And prepare myself to carry the sound of your screams against my heart for the rest of my days.*

Chapter Fourteen

That afternoon, Serena wore a crème colored silk with a jade overskirt to embody spring itself. Delilah had invited her on an open carriage ride to view a local flower fair and their maids were to accompany them. As they collected on Southgate Hall's front steps, it was Serena's first chance to meet Miss Dell.

Serena made a quick study of the girl, unsettled by her previous assumptions that this girl would be some sturdy country thing. Dell was a fine-boned creature, petite and slight and reminded Serena far too closely of her own beloved Pepper.

It was irrational to embrace the comparison and allow her imagination to too easily place Pepper into a hundred harmful fantasies but…the impulse was difficult to overcome.

*I dislike my plan more and more for—*

"Forgive me, my lady!" Dell took a quick step back, her color turning an awkward hue. "I…I feel unwell!"

"Oh! Dell, see to yourself and—no need to apologize!" Delilah said quickly as her maid fled back into the house to avoid being sick in front of the others.

Pepper shook her head. "That won't go unnoticed for long," she sighed. "They're already watching her close downstairs. I think Mrs. Watson fears it but she's too kind to say."

"Oh!" Delilah exclaimed. "Oh, god!"

"Fear not, Mrs. Osborne!" Serena comforted her friend and gave Pepper a warning look. "Pepper speaks with candor and not malice. It's one of the things I both prize in her but also dread."

Pepper smiled. "It's my best quality, Mrs. Osborne. But don't you worry. I'll make sure to complain of a touch of an ill stomach and make sure there's not a raised eyebrow to be seen!"

Delilah smiled in return. "Thank you. Thank you so much."

The coachmen came away from checking the horses and the women immediately altered the course of their conversation.

"We should be off then?" Serena asked.

"I'm—I'm not sure if I should leave Dell in such a state." Delilah hesitated.

"I can remain behind and see to her," Pepper offered. "I don't mind. Besides, what do I know of flowers from weeds?"

"That's kind of you. But only if you're sure…"

"I'd feel better staying. No need to spoil your outing, Mrs. Osborne. She's in good hands." Pepper was openly more cheered to stay than she'd been eyeing the horse and carriage and bobbed a curtsey before skipping back toward the servant's entrance to the kitchens.

Serena smiled. "Pepper is terrified of horses, Mrs. Osborne. I think Dell has earned her eternal gratitude for this last minute change in our plans."

"Would there be room for an additional change to your itinerary, ladies?" Phillip's voice carried from the top of the steps. "Perhaps you would care for an escort on your adventure?"

Delilah's surprise was total. "Phillip! I apologize! I never thought to invite you to…such a mundane and feminine outing."

"Your company is never mundane and what man doesn't revel in feminine outings? If only for the view they afford me into a secret world I can only guess at." Phillip came down the steps, the tailored lines of his coat accenting his height and the broadness of his shoulders. "And you never know! Gypsies and ruffians may have overrun the village in the dark of night and you may be grateful for my presence."

Serena had to bite the inside of her cheek to keep from laughing. "Oh, my! Well, if it wards off highwaymen and warlocks, I don't see how we thought to go without you, sir!"

"Just so!" Phillip touched the brim of his hat. "I am at your service."

"What fun!" Delilah's acceptance was the final stroke of approval he needed. He helped them both climb up into the carriage and then took the seat across from them. Skirts were arranged, parasols unfurled and they set off, as merry a party as ever.

Within minutes, Phillip had his cousin giggling so hard that Serena nearly had to pat her on the back for fear that she would not catch her breath.

"I never did!" Delilah protested weakly.

"I have witnesses that I can gather written and sworn statements from to the contrary!" he said with a wry grin. "I was twelve and it was indelibly carved into my memory. You with a hundred apples piled into your skirts that you could only carry by holding the hem up above your head in a giant bag—which naturally interfered with your ability to see where you were going!"

"Delilah!" Serena pretended shock. "Did you walk about with your skirts pulled up over your head?"

"It was a dozen apples and I…I do not remember the…exact method of cartage." Delilah blushed. "I had just gotten a pet rabbit and as I recall, the notion of giving it apples overwhelmed my reason. I was…very excited."

"It was nearly a bushel and enough for a warren of rabbits," Phillip amended. "You were so sweet, Delilah. Tearfully trying not to drop a single one and completely trapped in that petticoat prison you'd constructed."

Serena theatrically reassessed him. "And *you* did nothing to help your dear cousin? What kind of foul bully were you, Sir Warrick? I am seeing you in a new light, sir."

"Ah! Now she has caught you out!" Delilah laughed. "He helped me! He caught the front hem of my dress and pulled it out behind him so we created a bit of a hammock between us, did we not?"

"We saved all the apples and a portion of your modesty," he admitted.

"And did your bunny enjoy the 'fruits of your labors'?" Serena asked.

"One or two," Delilah replied. "The rest went into pies, crisps and sauces for the kitchen."

"So you admit it then," Phillip leaned forward with a wink. "It was far more than a dozen, wasn't it, Cousin Delilah?"

She blushed again and nodded happily. "As you say. But I will take the exact count to my grave!"

And so it went. Serena struggled not to be dazzled and charmed as Sir Phillip Warrick relaxed in her presence, enjoyed benign stories of his childhood with his cousin and revealed what unguarded moments with him could be. This was Phillip without a care in the world.

The potential was intoxicating but also tortuous.

For here was the man she'd loved and lost. Here, the conversations she'd imagined they would have had as their lives unfolded. Except that in her daydreams, they would have added their own stories to the tapestry, their own children, and their own laughter to the landscape of their days.

Lady Serena Wellcott no longer wasted time with daydreams and had long since banished the memory of those imaginary landscapes. She forced herself to recall that when her plans unfolded to destroy James, there was no telling what his reaction would be.

And there was no turning back.

"Ah! The flower fair! We have arrived, at last!" Delilah clapped her hands as the carriage pulled to a stop.

Phillip climbed down first and helped his cousin to her feet and then reached back up to Serena. "My lady?"

"Is it safe?" She pretended to eye the crowd of local gardeners and proud matrons with their tables of flower arrangements with great suspicion. "Those tablecloths certainly look long enough to cover at least three gypsies apiece if you fear an ambush."

"Stay close by my side, Lady Wellcott, and no harm will come to you." Phillip held out his outstretched hand and she took it as seriously as a queen accepting a scepter.

"So you say but we shall see."

A circumspect walk about the tables was as diverting as any as the cousins openly enjoyed the day. Serena took in the beauty of the local blooms and tried to keep her spirit from withering at the growing sense that the day was the last of its kind for her.

*One perfect day where things are light and easy between us, before all is lost and forever changed.*

"Congratulations on your winning ribbon, madam," Serena said, admiring the ribbon tied to the table of a particularly large basket of dahlias. "They are lovely."

The woman behind the table curtsied, her color deepening to match her flowers. "Ain't ye kind, yer ladyship!"

Delilah stepped up to add her own praise to the exchange. "You will have everyone in the guild begging you for cuttings, Mrs. Bell, including me! They are so vibrant!"

Mrs. Bell curtsied again, openly thrilled at the attention. "I've a secret or two I shall keep, I think! But weren't the Delaford's gardener spitting mad to see that blue ribbon land on me pretties!"

Delilah nodded, lowering her voice discreetly. "Mrs. Delaford *always* wins the blue ribbon."

"Well, not *always*," Serena noted. "And what a pleasant turn of events!"

"Pleasant and well deserved," Delilah echoed. "Congratulations, Mrs. Bell."

As they walked on, Delilah took Phillip's arm. "Your duty seems clear, Phillip."

"Does it?" he asked.

"You must check under the Mrs. Bell's tablecloth for saboteurs."

He smiled as Serena gestured toward a table covered in red roses.

"The Delafords have quite the look for hardened villains." Serena moved her parasol to block them from view. "I shouldn't be surprised if she has a stiletto in that bodice."

"Oh!" Delilah gasped, covering her mouth to keep from laughing.

Phillip stole a peek and then nodded his head. "She could have a longsword in *that* bodice."

"Phillip Warrick!" Poor Delilah had had all the mischief she could manage for one afternoon and struck her cousin in the shoulder. "Behave!"

"I?" he asked in mock astonishment. "Lady Wellcott was the one who—"

"What kind of gentleman deflects the blame to an innocent woman?" Serena interrupted him, folding her parasol in indignation. "What is this?"

Phillip bowed his head, immediately acknowledging that he was outnumbered and unlikely to carry the day. "I apologize. I was overzealous in my guard duty and may have inhaled a strange combination of poppies to overtake my senses." He put a hand to his head. "I think I should sit down before I add to my doom."

"I think we have all had enough of flowers for today." Delilah announced. "Let's head home."

They began to walk back to the waiting carriage in the lane by the church yard. "And you, Lady Wellcott? Have you had enough of flowers today?" Phillip asked.

"I suppose so if—"

Phillip held out a small nosegay tied with a green ribbon that matched her ensemble. "Say you have not, Lady Wellcott."

Serena eyed the forget-me-nots, honey flowers and everlastings, traditionally symbols of love ever faithful and steadfast, love that did not fade despite adversity and a love never forgotten.

*Damn it.*

In front of Delilah, she felt trapped. To refuse him seemed too brusque a response after the delights of the day but to accept them felt like a bitter betrayal. He'd vowed to keep their secret yet now he was standing before her like a suitor on a penny card. Serena let out a long slow breath. "How...charming."

"You can take them to your maid," he said evenly, a gleam in his eyes. "So that she will not feel too badly for missing the day." He turned to Delilah and held out an identical nosegay. "Here. For your Dell."

*Well played. Wretched man!*

"Aren't you sweet!" Delilah exclaimed and took the flowers from his hand. "What a thoughtful thing to do!"

"Yes," Serena conceded. "Very thoughtful." She took the miniature bouquet from him and inhaled the delicate fragrances. She glanced up at him through her eyelashes and caught him staring at her with raw hunger and appreciation. Serena smiled at him and let the moment pass.

*One man's victory is another woman's defeat.*

The return ride to the house was a slightly more subdued journey as Serena clutched her nosegay and pretended that love could last.

"You are warming to each other," Delilah noted after they'd arrived at Southgate Hall and Lady Wellcott had retreated to her rooms. Delilah had invited Phillip for a quick turn in the gardens and as always, he seemed incapable of refusing her.

"We are." Phillip agreed, trailing his hands across the top of the lavender blooms along the graveled walkway. He wasn't sure what else he could say without betraying that heat had never been lacking in his relationship with Raven Wells. "Lady Wellcott is a remarkable woman."

"She is," Delilah said and shifted her parasol to block the sun. "I am happy you have secured a cease-fire."

"Your husband is ecstatic. I only wish he'd stop grinning at me like an ape when he thinks no one is looking." Phillip shuddered. "How is it that even when things go well, James finds a way to toss a bit of dirt into the pudding?"

"I'm sure he believes it to be a form of encouragement," Delilah said softly.

"I apologize, cousin. I did not mean to speak ill of your husband."

"Family has a way of provoking the worst in us." She touched his arm. "And if I have been a trial to you, Phillip, then I should be the one to apologize."

"You? Never!" He covered her fingers with his. "Delilah, I think your soft nature if confronted by the Devil himself would inspire you to offer him a shady place to sit and inquire into his health."

"Oh, dear! I will have to amend my ways and take on a more foreboding manner." Delilah laughed.

"But what trial did you speak of?"

"I pushed you to make amends with Lady Wellcott but…" Delilah's steps slowed to a stop to face him. "My friend is not a woman to be toyed with, Phillip. If you mean to simply flirt to appease the situation, or make light of the pursuit then you will have bitten off far more than you can safely chew."

"What do you know of Lady Wellcott? What are you saying?"

"I am saying that of all the women I know, she will not stomach a man's deceit." Delilah shook her head as if to clear her mind. "Are you playacting, Phillip? To make James happy?"

"No. I am not playacting."

"Then you genuinely care for Lady Wellcott?"

"Beyond measure."

Delilah sighed. "Well, that is something." They continued down the path away from the house. "I won't meddle, cousin. Once upon a time, I imagined that I was a gifted matchmaker with a keen knowledge of the human heart…"

"And now?"

She looked at him, a haunted shadow drifting across her eyes. "I know nothing of love, cousin. Absolutely nothing."

She turned and left him on the walkway, and Phillip swallowed hard at the sight of her as a small and solitary figure returning to the carved stone Georgian home behind them like a woman marching toward the gallows.

It was a quiet party that night at dinner. Delilah made no effort to recount the day once her husband derided their destination and mocked Phillip's attendance at what he deemed a peasant's floral parade.

Serena watched her host closely, making note of his deteriorating social skills and surly disposition. If celibacy had contributed to his mood this quickly, it was hard not to feel more and more confident in his self-destruction. Even as Phillip tried to cheer the man with talk of business or tales of London, Serena felt like a woman viewing a dark improvisation.

*Time is going fast.*

*Too fast.*

After dinner, everyone pleaded fatigue and Serena excused herself to retreat to her room. She prepared for bed and then stood at her window for a while to watch the stars rise. The moon was waning but still bright enough to compete with the fiery diamonds of the night sky.

Phillip's soft knock was not unexpected but she closed her eyes, tasting reluctance. She opened the door slowly without stepping back to let him in. "No."

His brow furrowed in confusion. "Serena? We had such a lovely day and—"

"Forgive me, Phillip. I…my head is pounding and I cannot think of…"

He yielded so gently it fueled her misery. "Of course." He leaned in to kiss her sweetly on her forehead. "Feel better, my love and sleep. Would you like platonic company to soothe your nerves or—"

She held up a hand to stop him. "You are being too kind, Sir Warrick. I cannot imagine admitting you to my bed only to require you to play nursemaid. Please. One night's respite and I will be restored. I swear it."

He smiled. "One night's respite."

He kissed her again, a platonic brush of his lips to hers that melted into a searing taste of desire before he lifted his head and stepped back in amazement. "I begin to see the dilemma you alluded to, Lady Wellcott."

"Good night, Sir Warrick."

"Good night, Serena."

She closed the door gently but with a firm hand, unwilling to risk standing there gazing at him to give in to temptation. The day had been rife with the strange bruises that came with every sweet look he'd favored her with and every gentle and unremarkable moment. Happiness she had shielded her heart from and shied from glancing at had invaded her realm without warning.

And God help her, she wasn't ready to mourn its loss.


Phillip walked down the hall with a quiet bounce in his step. True, he'd been sent off without much amorous relief but the prize he wanted most of all was within sight.

Because when he'd stepped forward to kiss her, he'd seen something that made her withdrawal palatable. On her vanity table in a small crystal vase filled with water to preserve it was the nosegay he'd given her and the meaning of the blooms echoed in his head with every footfall.

*Enduring love, sweet and secret.*

Chapter Fifteen

Serena stole a few moments of privacy in the ground floor music
room. A small pianoforte beckoned her to sit and she gave in to
the impulse. She plucked out a few chords and smiled at the
memory of her first lessons with the vicar's wife. Mrs. Gilchrist
had always smelled of rosewater and though Serena could barely
summon her face or her hair color to mind, she remembered with
perfect clarity the beauty of her hands on the piano keys and the
gentle melody of her voice.

Serena began to play, then added her voice to the
performance.

*"My love, a lily grows, without sunlight*

*Without sighs.*

*I seek to hear him on the garden path*

*And in the flowered lanes.*

*My love, swiftly flees, without a sign*

*Of his return and I am left to plead.*

*To find him in the meadow fair*

*Or in the gentle plains.*

*My love, another seeks to hold,*

*My heart abandoned there."*

"It's as if an angel had come into my house," James said as he applauded from the doorway.

Serena stood, swallowing displeasure at the intrusion. "I am not much of a singer, Mr. Osborne, but I thank you for the compliment."

"I meant to collect Phillip for an outing we'd planned but I was drawn to the sound of your voice." He crossed toward her. "You should sing for our small company after dinner tonight."

"I am not a performer, Mr. Osborne."

"What? It is not unseemly at a small house party to be entertained so! A guest should earn their keep and I am a man eager for diversion." He smiled. "It's not as if I've committed the offense of asking how much you charge for a song! Though I have yet to meet a woman who could not name a price when pushed to it." He winked at her slyly before he openly made an appreciative survey of the rise of her breasts above the cut of her bodice. "What is a coin or two for lively entertainment between the sexes?"

Serena tipped her head to one side, studying the man. "Mr. Osborne, I wonder. I once knew a man who would blurt out the most extraordinary things. Horrible things sometimes but then at other times, it would be poetry and lengthy odes to make people laugh."

"Was he a great man?" James asked.

"Not at all," she said simply. "He wore rags and mumbled to himself from a corner of the pub and everyone who knew him credited him with having no wits at all. And I would have agreed until I spotted the game."

"What was the game?"

"He knew exactly what he was saying and tempered every outburst to those within its hearing. Ladies and the older men of the priory would throw coins if he quoted the bible or spouted poetry. Gentlemen would pay him to leave if he made a jolly lively show of it and the rough locals would slip him a coin for his most ribald pieces."

"So he had his wits."

"His wits *and* a plan." She nodded slowly. "He lived very well."

"It is an interesting tale, Lady Wellcott. But I am not sure why you've shared it with me."

"I shared it because I am determined to see if you have your wits only, or your wits *and* a plan—or neither."

James smile died in an awkward slow demise. "Do you think to mock me to my face, Lady Wellcott? Is this what you consider a grand jest?"

"No, sir. I meant only to reassure myself that when you allude to some grotesque belief that all women are nothing better than whores that if it is just the impulse of your foul humor, I should know to slap your face. Or that if it was your hope to shock me, then I must try to understand what gain could be secured. Or were you speaking without thought or plan?" She held her ground. "For then the insult is one I will ignore, the way I would ignore the mindless barking of a dog."

James' gaze narrowed, a flare of disgust in his eyes. "How sensitive you are, Lady Wellcott! A compliment about your voice and an invitation to share your talents with my wife and cousin and…you bristle like a cat thrown in a bathtub!"

Serena smiled sympathetically. "My claws are sharp. A good thing I never lash out without warning and how fortunate I am that you are so understanding."

James crossed his arms. "I understand you well enough. I am honored to have a woman of your station under my roof, but I don't care if you are a crown princess. At the end of the day, you are just a woman and I—I am the master in this house."

Serena nodded, a wicked gleam in her eyes. "What did you say, Mr. Osborne? I couldn't hear you over the sound of all that barking."

It nearly ended, right then and there, as James hands curled into fists and Serena sensed that she had pushed him far enough to achieve her aims.

*He'll strike and it's all to the good. Pepper will be out of it and he'll commit an act of violence he cannot retract.*

"James!" Phillip called out from the doorway. "I thought you were going to meet me on the steps. Your land manager, Mr. Chilton, is already outside." He stopped abruptly. "Oh, Lady Wellcott! I didn't see you there."

James turned away from her, his arms dropping. "I'm sorry, cousin. I was distracted by Lady Wellcott's riveting presence and forgot the time."

"I cannot blame you then," Phillip conceded with a smile. "Do you mind if I pull him away, Lady Wellcott?"

"Not at all," she said in a level tone that conveyed nothing of her frustration.

*Damn the timing!*

James retreated without looking back and Serena watched him stride out, his brisk steps betraying his unhappy state.

*God, how simple might that have been? Seconds more and I would have had him!*

*Best to warn Mrs. Osborne that she must lock her bedroom door and make sure that the maids are warned of their master's foul mood. But I don't think I should tell her that this is the last day.*

*It's too close and nothing can tip our hand.*

*Damn it to hell!*

Chapter Sixteen

After dispatching Pepper with messages for the housekeeper and for Mrs. Osborne, Serena paced alone in the garden under the covered walkway along the wall. She liked the shadowed quiet of the place and the privacy it offered. The vines had flowered even more since her arrival, creating a haven away from the house to think.

She regretted the exchange with Mr. Osborne but only because it hadn't yielded a well-timed assault on the ground floor of the man's home. She was inherently confident that they'd have been discovered before he'd murdered her.

*Certainly plenty to break in that room to herald distress and bring the house crashing in...*

Serena pressed her fingers against her closed eyes, willing the wall of anxiety to retreat. Bruises were easy to endure, if they were hers. But after staring down James Osborne, she dreaded the notion of Pepper playing such a part.

*Perhaps I can alter the plan...now that I have his attention and his blood is stirred, can I divert him to—*

"Lady Wellcott."

She pivoted to absorb Phillip's second ill-timed entrance of the day. "Sir Warrick. I thought you were out with Mr. Osborne on some grand adventure."

"My horse became lame and I made my excuses," he stepped forward, holding out a small basket as if it were a peace offering. "Yours is the company I would rather keep."

"Really?" She smiled. "How flattering to be chosen over a survey of tenant cottages and weaver shops!"

He laughed. "I knew you would grasp the significance of my sacrifice!"

"What is in this basket, Sir Warrick?"

"It is a wicked offering, Lady Wellcott." He lifted the cloth inside to reveal a bottle of wine and two cut crystal glasses. "I am tired of tea."

"Blasphemy!" Serena gasped. "The scandal, sir!"

"I am at the mercy of your discretion, Lady Wellcott."

"There is nothing to be done for it, Phillip. Open the bottle and we shall have to face it together." Serena made her way to a low bench at the far end of the path. "Here, do your worst."

He sat next to her, spread out the small cloth between them and opened the wine to pour them each a glass of liquid the color of rubies. "Why does wine always seem so much more luxurious when it is pilfered from someone else's cellars?"

"Ah! One of life's great mysteries!" Serena lifted the glass to study the facets of color. "Is it the sin that makes it sweeter?"

"I might toast that." He held up his glass and she kissed hers against it, the bell like tone making a pretty finish to the gesture. "To the sweeter sin."

"The sweetest sins of all," she echoed softly.

The wine was bright and strong in her mouth, the flavor softening on her tongue as she inhaled the fragrance. She shook her head slowly. "God, I remember when wine and all spirits were so forbidden to me!"

She looked at Phillip, aware that she'd nearly spoken Trent's name aloud for it was her guardian's one act of strict discipline to not allow her to taste anything strong under his roof. The man had forbidden nothing else—applauding her every feminine impulse and imaginative thought in the twisted guidance of a man who wished to bring up the "perfect woman". If only she'd known that perfection's price would be her own soul...

She leaned over to kiss him, tasting the echo of wine on his lips and tongue and wondering if he was experiencing the same on hers. She sighed and the kiss deepened.

*Sweet taste of sin.*

"I hate him so much that I fear you can smell it on my skin, Serena." Phillip downed his glass and then set it aside, the jovial tone of the moment lost.

"I know." She sighed and straightened her shoulders. "I don't think you can avoid it any longer, Sir Warrick."

"Avoid what?"

"Go on. It will eat at you like a cancer until you face it. You must demand the answers you need. Yes?"

"Tell me. Tell me what happened at Oakwell seven years ago."

She bristled at the command. "Trent used to say that. *Tell me.* God, he loved to hear a good story, didn't he?" Serena held her own elbows and then leaned back against the wall of vines, settling in like a queen holding court. "Oddly, I find myself averse to telling any man anything. But I did invite this, didn't I?"

"Please, Serena. Tell me your side of it. After we parted ways, I came back for you. The weather slowed me down and I lost time. Too much time. But there was no sign of where you had gone." He lifted the bottle to pour them each another drink. "I lost weeks searching until I became convinced that you were irrevocably gone from me and from life itself."

Serena went still but then took the offered drink. She looked up at him to study him, the grip on the crystal glass in her hand growing nerveless. "You truly came back for me?"

He nodded. "You'd emptied your cases by the side of the road and even your bonnets had blown into the hedges. It was a...miserable scene."

"That it was." She squared her shoulders. "How could it be otherwise?"

"Damn it. If I'm to own my mistakes, then is this not a chance to ensure I am schooled in full measure? Here is your chance, Lady Wellcott. Punish me with the truth."

"And what makes me think you'd believe that truth? That you wouldn't insulate your pride with the poison of Trent's making? For I of all people know how insidious that poison can be, Sir Warrick. I, who was baptized in it, without my knowledge."

He bowed his head, absorbing that defeat was all too possible. "Please."

"Very well. But I need to pace about if I'm to get through it all. So, I'm asking you to sit and allow me to move as I must."

"Granted."

True to his word, he kept his seat as she stood to take command of the shaded walk. "There was a touch of truth in that letter, Sir Warrick. I was an illegitimate child abandoned at birth. I was given at my father's request to a vicar and his wife. It was an idyllic beginning and I am forever grateful for their care."

"But Trent?"

"The reverend and his wife were killed in an epidemic and I was placed into a home for orphaned and unwanted children. My father wasn't immediately aware of the change and then asked a trusted friend, the Earl of Trent, to track down his lost daughter. Trent offered to not only find me but "see to me". Generous of him, yes?"

"Oh, hell."

"Ah, yes! You can see the shape of the rest of it. Trent already apparently had some grievance against you and decided that a young girl with good bloodlines and a clear complexion was just the thing. All I knew was that I had been plucked from a nightmare and my guardian was my savior. He shared nothing of his plans, nothing of his dark notions and I—I obliviously enjoyed buying bonnets and silks, devoured what education I desired and dreamed of a life where I would never be cold or hungry again."

Phillip's color changed as the story he'd begged her for now began to batter his conscience. But he said nothing.

"I fell in love with a handsome man who fell off of his horse. I fell into his arms at every opportunity because I didn't know what it was to fear. I gave myself to that man without a nod to self-preservation, so sure of the wisdom of my own heart and convinced that the happiness he gave me would sustain me for centuries." Serena took a good swallow from her wine, savoring the taste but also the agony in Phillip's eyes. "Then he swept me away with a vow to marry me. And then he threw me from his carriage in the rain."

"Shit."

"Yes. Exactly as one would scrape dung off your shoes." She nodded. "But here's the bit you were particularly interested in, correct? Some recounting of the horror of screaming after that carriage, of crying your name until my voice was a ragged ruin, of kneeling in the mud and begging a merciful God to strike me down?"

"No."

She smiled, emptied her glass in one elegant draw and then set it aside on the bench next to him. "Oh, don't lose your courage now! Here is where the story becomes a little more interesting, Sir Warrick. Because God didn't end Raven Wells. I did. I left her by the side of the road and determined that never again would I trust to Fate. I walked down that road in the opposite direction that you had flown and made my way over several days to my father's estate."

"Your father? You knew who your father was all along?"

"It wasn't hard to guess, but when he made an appearance at the county dance and spoke to me, I knew my suspicions were true." She moved to the end of the covered arches and looked out into the garden. "What a bedraggled thing I must have been by the time I rang the bell at his servants' entrance. I gave my name and offered my services as the lowest of the low, as a scullery maid or kitchen girl. I bid the housekeeper tell their master that Raven Wells would be eternally grateful to sleep on his stone floors and had no hope beyond that shelter. And God help me, I meant it."

"A scullery maid," he repeated in a horrified whisper. "I cannot bear to think of it."

She laughed. "There are worse things, Sir Warrick, to be in this world. And since you'd already proclaimed me a whore, I'm surprised you aren't more pleased to hear that I aspired to a more honorable career."

"I was wrong."

"Of course you were." She looked at him with disgust. "How is it that you still look surprised when you say those words, Sir Warrick?" She shifted her gaze back to the window. "I never scrubbed a single copper pot. The instant the duke realized I had landed at his doorstep, I was brought upstairs to meet him again."

"A duke?!" Phillip looked like a man who had seen a ghost. "My god, it's a penny dreadful."

"He is—and the esteemed author of my present existence. The duke was horrified to learn of his friend's betrayal of my care and the true nature of my "rescue". He'd have struck Trent down himself, but I—I begged for mercy. Not out of some generous Christian spirit but because even then, I knew…I knew that I wanted the pleasure of it for myself. But that is for another day. Let's see. Where did I leave off? Yes. My father took me in and I was once more relieved of catastrophe to land in silks and feathers."

Phillip said nothing more and she was glad for it.

"Only this time, my savior had no dark plans for me; only paternal care. The Duke of Northland has no direct heirs. Even so, naturally he could not acknowledge me publicly as his, but a title was purchased along with token holdings, a massive fortune set aside and respectability carved out with his connections and cemented by a year abroad. I became Lady Serena Wellcott." Serena circled back to take a seat next to him. "But every good story must have a twist, Sir Warrick. Can you guess at mine?"

He shook his head. "No. Abandoned, orphaned, used in a wicked scheme, ruined by a rogue only to land in the care of a duke and given a new identity? Haven't there already been too many twists and turns?"

"Hardly. For you see, now the dark plans and wicked schemes are mine. I am the mistress of my days and nights. And revenge, I have learned, can be an elegant and satisfying thing."

"You don't mean that. Not after experiencing all of that at the hands of Trent and—"

"And at your hands?" She let him shift in his chair in the glorious discomfort of the truth. "Do you not remember Lady Morley?"

"The wife who ran away from her husband..."

"I helped engineer her entire escape and Lord Morley never did find her." She leaned forward as her passion for the subject seized her. "It was power. Power I had never known before! I had aided a woman in need and as time passed, it came to me that the world may have a place for me after all. I would assist women who had no recourse to justice, no chance for happiness, or who had been wronged. I would make it my life's work to balance the scales by using all the lessons of my youth, the talents honed by tragedy and plenty alike, and I would see to it that no woman who petitioned for mercy went unheard."

Phillip sat up straighter. "Why are you here, Serena?"

A flash of anxiety whipped up her spine at the realization that she may have said too much but Serena smiled at him as if he'd asked about the weather. "Because Mrs. Osborne is your cousin and I heard a rumor that you had been invited to this little country gathering, Sir Warrick. It has been a few years and I decided that I was ready to see what kind of man you'd become."

"And seek your revenge?"

She slowly reclined back in her chair, her gaze shimmering with confidence in her sexual prowess. "Frightened, Sir Warrick?"

"I am not frightened of you. Should I fear?"

"No, not directly."

"Then you *were* here to hurt my family in some petty strike at—"

"Don't be an idiot, Phillip. I've already told you. I'm no brutish henchmen to prowl around the halls and injure your relatives without cause." She rolled her eyes. "God, why do men have no imagination?"

Serena stood in an elegant maneuver that barely gave him time to get his feet underneath him before he realized that this time she was not pacing but abandoning their vine covered grotto.

"Then, what *are* your intentions now, Lady Wellcott?" he asked.

She blinked at him, a flirtatious flutter of eyelashes that any courtesan would have applauded. "What kind of villain would I be if I announced such a thing? Perhaps you must seduce it out of me, sir. What say you?"

Phillip's mouth fell open in shock but he struggled to recover his composure. "I'd say that was a fool's challenge."

She pressed her lips into a pout. "Am I not desirable, Sir Warrick?"

"You are more than desirable."

Her chin lifted. "You want to be punished? Then come, Sir Warrick. Prove what kind of man you've become. One that is ruled by fear to cower at the brush of a woman's skirts? Or one who is willing to make amends and take what is offered?" She stood as if to go. "Make no mistake. I am not attracted to fools."

He caught her wrist and thwarted her escape. "You are not a villain, Lady Wellcott. And I am not a fool." She held her breath and he went on. "I am sorry, Serena. I am completely sorry for all the pain I caused you that fateful day. For the lies I swallowed and the callous heartless actions I took. For the suffering, for the years lost and for every stupid instance that cheated me out of the pure happiness and joy that you fearlessly gifted me with." He kissed her hands then turned them over to place another reverent kiss on the tender flesh of her palms. "I am in the Duke of Northland's debt but not for feathers and silk and fortunes…but because he saved you when I was too blind and stupid to be the man that you deserved. My God, I am so, so sorry."

She bowed her head, closing her eyes as the balm of his words finally edged close to the worst of her wounds. *There. The apology I dreamt of and longed for…*

*Except it may all be too late.*

She looked back up at him. "Thank you for that."

"Come to me tonight, Serena."

"Yes." Her eyes filled with unshed tears but she averted her face before he could see them. "I will come to you tonight."

He released her hand and she walked back toward the house as gracefully as she could, despite the lash of her emotions that urged her to run.

*Yes, one last time.*

*Because tomorrow it all comes to head one way or another and it is over.*

*Tomorrow, it will rain.*

Chapter Seventeen

She waited until midnight before she came to his rooms.

*I have changed into a woman he doesn't really know.*

*A woman he isn't likely to want to know.*

*But there is time for one last night to embrace the lie and*

*pretend that it isn't too late.*

She knocked softly and entered quickly without waiting for
his answer. He was there, just as she'd known he would be,
standing at the center of the room. A single candle was lit by the
bed to cast a beautiful glow throughout the space and giving it a
magical quality.

"You came."

She smiled. "Did you have any doubts that I would?"

"I'd be a fool not to entertain the possibility that a woman
can always change her mind," he replied with a smile.

"Ah! You're learning the way of it now."

He approached her slowly, tipping her head up slowly to kiss her. "I am lucky to have such a beautiful tutor."

He teased her with the whisper of a kiss and Serena nearly cried at what his touch foretold.

*Not slow. Please, god...not slow.*

She wasn't sure her heart could survive it. She wanted him to rush her, to race her to the finish and be done with it; as if the pain of a knife's thrust would be lessened with speed.

She tried to hurry him, to overwhelm him. She pushed the robe from his shoulders to reveal his naked form and knelt to incite him to action, aware that her mouth against his sex would weave a spell to wrench control from his hands.

His cock came to life at the first brush of her hot breath across the silky soft skin covering his hardening shaft. Serena admired the vigor of his body and the taut evidence that she alone commanded him. She kissed the darkening tip, delving her tongue against him to taste the first pearl of moisture that demonstrated his readiness. She found the sensitive ridge underneath his length and then pulled him inside the velvet pocket of her mouth, drawing against his strength with a gentle assault of tongue and teeth. He sighed at her touch, holding as still as he could to allow her to play as she wished.

Serena tightened her grip, eliciting pleasure from the way his body responded, alternating each stroke of her fingers with a long sweet kiss across his flesh until he was moaning for more.

He stepped away without warning, gently disengaging her from the game. Phillip reached under her arms and lifted her to her feet. "Come, Lady Wellcott." He began to lead her to his bed. "Come to me. Why hurry, my love? We have all the time we need. All the time in the world…"

Words failed her but she took his hand and followed him to the bed. He climbed up onto the mattress and she quickly pulled off her nightgown to toss it on the floor before joining him. Serena crawled up, deliberately exaggerating her movements like a cat, drawing his eyes to her curves and allowing her long black hair to trail up his frame as she carefully landed on top of him.

Then for a strange second, she forgot her seductive plan to push him and lost her place. She covered him with her body, placing one of her cars against his chest.

"What are you doing?" he asked.

"Shh! I'm listening to your heartbeat," she confessed softly. She closed her eyes to try to absorb the strong thrum and thud of his heart beneath her as if to draw it into her soul. It was a sound that mesmerized her and made her wonder if she would ever again indulge in dreams where Phillip Warrick's heart beat with love for her.

Tears slipped from her eyes and fell onto his skin and he jolted at the sensation. "Serena! Are you crying?"

"No! Don't be foolish!" The denial would have been effective if not for the hiccup that followed it and the clear evidence on her face that she was a liar.

He'd shifted her off to change places with her before she could stop him, cradling her in his arms against the soft mattress beneath her. "What troubles you?"

"The moon," she whispered. "Kiss me."

The look of confusion on his face was priceless but he complied, kissing her with renewed fervor. Where he led, she followed. In an ageless dance, they explored and teased, gave and took pleasure in equal measure and then forgot to measure anything at all, not even time.

The candlelight transformed them both into creatures of golden light and darkest shadows. Her skin was warmed by his hands and every path of his hands coaxed her to life as if she couldn't move unless he was there to inspire her blood to flow or her heart to beat. It was an intoxicating paradox as she was the siren that danced to the music of his groans astride his hips but Serena knew that it was not Phillip who was drowning.

Her body welcomed him and she shuddered at the power of it.

He pulled her down into the bed, their primal ritual taking a slow turn from want to need. Serena spread her thighs apart even wider to urge him on and then arched her back as every line blurred between victory and surrender, between the past and the present.

Her release built slowly this time, as if her body knew what she couldn't acknowledge, that letting go meant losing far more than a moment's control this time. Some stubborn part of her resisted it but she was no match for Phillip's patient assault on her senses. His body was a relentless and impossibly sexy opponent as one gentle tactic after another finally exhausted her defenses.

When it was close, Serena clung to him, tears pressed from eyes as frustration yielded to an exquisite pang of shuddering ecstasy and agonizingly slow waves that made her shudder and buck against him. She cried out at the strange sense that her soul was caught in the tangle of this and that she had just given up something she could never have again.

And she hated him for it.

And she loved him for it.

*Dreams of Oakwell gave way to a strange return to the Greenwood Home for orphaned and unwanted children. She'd pushed through the doors to the solarium and ended up in the courtyard of the hell of her childhood. But this time, they'd chained her to the flagstones and somewhere Pepper was in danger. Pepper was screaming because a monster was raping her.*

*Raven was trapped. Trapped in the rain. Helpless.*

*And the flagstones turned to mud…and Pepper stopped screaming.*

*And that was so much worse.*

Awareness came hard as she sat up in a cold sweat, the terror of her nightmare seizing her by the throat and choking her. She slowly caught her breath and accepted that she had unwittingly fallen asleep in the bed next to Phillip. Serena waited to see if she had disturbed him with it, but mercifully he slumbered on, unaware of her.

She shook her head to try to banish fear. *Oh, God. What if I have crossed a new line and have far more to lose than to gain if I surpass the evil deeds of the villains of my childhood in my reach for justice?*

*What kind of demon puts an innocent in harm's way?*

It was too dark to really see Phillip's face and she was grateful for that one merciful detail. Serena slid cautiously from his bed, gathered her things, and slipped from his room, a refugee from her own past.

Chapter Eighteen

"You seem distracted, Lady Wellcott?" Phillip asked. "Did you

not sleep well?"

It was a wicked tease since he knew very well how she had

slept. But it wasn't the lack of sleep or erotic tangle he evoked

when he looked at her. Pepper's fleeting encounter with Mr.

Osborne and her own knowledge of how close the man was to

losing control heralded danger. She walked into the dining room

to join the others for breakfast, but found her steps turning uneven

as she became aware that their host was not in his chair at the head

of the table.

"I slept like a babe," she said, then shifted in her chair to

address Delilah. "Is your husband not joining us?"

Delilah shook her head. "He should be here any moment."

Phillip spoke as he retook his own seat. "I saw him upstairs earlier and he said something about a headache. Said he was going to take a powder and rest and that we shouldn't wait for him."

"Oh." Serena began to take a cup of coffee and then stopped, abruptly setting her cup aside. She hadn't seen him upstairs and there was no cause to fear.

*Except…*

*It's nothing. But why is my mouth dry? Why do I have the worst feeling? Pepper is upstairs in my bedroom and if he waited to see me leave…*

She stood. "If you'll excuse me. I meant to take a walk after breakfast and just realized I left my parasol upstairs."

"No need to race for it. I'll just ring to have Dell bring it down for—"

"No reason to bother her." She didn't linger for a debate on the inefficiency or complex protocol that meant staying in the dining room. "I'll be back shortly."

Her pace increased with every step she took. The planned ambush of Osborne now felt like a flimsy construct and all she could think of was Pepper. Memories of Pepper when she was all of five years old and looking to Raven for protection and solace in that damp dark hellhole. Pepper who had never questioned her and never faulted a friend who asked her to risk all in a quest for vengeance.

*Pepper! What have I done?*

She tried to shake off her fears. This was likely to end in laughter as Pepper mocked her surge of over-protectiveness but Raven knew that her plans had changed. She would find another way to bring Osborne down without—

A muffled cry through her bedroom door ended the train of her thoughts instantly.

She seized the door handle only to realize it was locked.

*No! Oh, no!*

She took one deep breath. *If I pound on the door, he is sure he's been discovered and all is lost. Oh, god. Hang on, Pepper!*

She ran from the door to the adjacent bedroom, sprinted into the dressing room and bolted toward the adjoining door that connected the two bedrooms. And just as she'd surmised, he'd bolted the door to the hall but a man like Osborne would never think to also lock a door used only by the maids.

She burst into the room and onto a scene from her worst nightmare. His pants were down around his knees and he'd forced Pepper face down onto the bed, her skirts pulled up to reveal her bare nethers. He half-turned in his shock at the intrusion, his thick erection bobbing beneath his belly while one hand was clamped viciously over Pepper's mouth to muffle her screams.

"Get off of her, you bastard!"

Serena rushed up to him without a single thought of strategy, her hands forming claws aimed at his eyes. He released Pepper's mouth and backhanded Serena before she could reach him to draw blood.

Stars of white hot pain danced in front of her eyes as she landed on the floor at his feet, her vision filled with the ugly sight of his wobbling red cock inches from her face.

Osborne laughed and reached down to grip his sex proudly, then released it to press his hips forward to show off his prowess. "Oh, get a good look, dear lady! You'll get your fill, soon enough!

So impatient!" He looked back to the bed, eyeing the object of his desire. "Just let me split this peach and we'll see if you don't—"

She reached up in one fluid stroke to retrieve the long six inch pin from its metal sheath hidden in her curls and drove it up deep into the wrinkled hairy fat pouch that held his balls. It was a single puncture that caused more pain than actual immediate damage but it was exactly what she'd intended. He screamed, a piercing high pitched wail that rivaled a banshee as he doubled over to cradle his insulted jewels. "You, bitch!"

"Help! He's at us!" Pepper screeched.

James glared at her maid in disgust unaware that Serena was sheathing the hair pin before he could see it in her hands. Serena kicked out with one heeled boot, squarely connecting with his bare inner thigh, pushing away from him to struggle to her feet. "Run, Pepper!"

"What is this, you witch?" James grabbed the woman closest to hand and the one he suspected had cut his balls open. His hand fisted into her hair with a roar, while the other involuntarily grabbed his injured flesh at the strain of holding her down. "What did you do?!"

"What's wrong, Mr. Osborne?" she whispered, wincing at the pain of his grip. "Was that you barking? I couldn't tell."

Fury overtook him and he lifted a closed fist readying to punch her before he realized that Pepper had indeed run. Sobs braying in innocent horror at what she had endured, she was fumbling with the lock on the bedroom door, hysterically seeking freedom and help in equal measure.

"Don't open that door! I'll snap your mistress' neck if you—"

Momentum carried Pepper past the threat before she understood his words, unlocking the heavy door and throwing it open only to be greeted by Phillip Warrick with Mrs. Osborne and three footmen along with a bewildered Mr. Clayborne holding a candelabra like a club.

"Oh, God! He—he's there! My mistress! Save my mistress!" Pepper cried as she fell against Phillip.

Serena's heart nearly broke that Pepper would even now, think of someone else's safety rather than her own. *Go on. Snap my neck and ensure that your own is broken by the hangman's noose!* Serena closed her eyes, calmly waiting for James Osborne to make his choice.

"Bitch!" Osborne growled as he released her, doing his best to stand away from her and then realizing his pants were still down. "She...lured me here!"

Serena looked at Phillip and the others, staggering to her feet and making no effort to hide the ruin of her right eye and cheek. "I came up for my parasol and found him in the midst of raping my maid! When I tried to stop him, he struck me and then threatened the same to me!"

Mrs. Osborne came quickly into the room to put an arm around her shoulders. "I am—so dreadfully sorry, Lady Wellcott! Your face!"

Serena reached up to touch her throbbing cheekbone and allowed the tears to start.

"You son of a bitch!" Phillip released Pepper so that he could murder his cousin's husband.

"I'm bleeding! That bitch! She cut me! She cut me!" Osborne held up a hand covered in blood, his eyes wide with primal masculine panic.

Phillip's steps slowed, his lip curling in a sardonic humor, but he seized James by the collar. "Cut you? With what?"

"I...I...don't know..." Osborne's fury wobbled as he fumbled between trying to pull up his britches and stem the flow of blood from an injury he couldn't see despite the agony that was undeniable.

"Do you have a weapon, Lady Wellcott?" Phillip asked.

She shook her head and held out her hands, fingers splayed to demonstrate their emptiness. "I am not in the habit of carrying weaponry, sir."

"Of course, you aren't. Which just leaves the matter of rape. Send for the constable, Delilah, and bid him to bring two strong men to cart a criminal from your house."

"No!" Osborne's fear took on a new dimension and a sharp edge at the realization that there were no less than six people looking on to the scene with calls echoing down the halls that were sure to summon every living soul in the house. "I—the scandal..."

"You should have thought of that before you assaulted a guest in our home!" Delilah said. "Before you assaulted a maid under my roof, you bastard!"

"J-just a maid! She wanted it! This is a terrible misunderstanding, Delilah. A man...I have my weaknesses and she...lured me...to....said her mistress was up...for it...as well..."

Pepper gasped at the suggestion and buried her face in her hands. Serena shifted away from Delilah to take Pepper into her arms. "Send for the doctor as well to see to my darling girl! But by all means, send for the constable. I will be the one to press charges and see this through! I know what I saw and will testify to the attempted rape and to your assault of my person." She glared at him defiantly. "Unless you care to claim that I somehow begged you to give me a black eye in the midst of this nightmare?"

Delilah slapped her husband so hard that the sound resembled a gunshot. "You're not a man. You rape a maid and think to blame her? You're a vile excuse for a human being!"

Her voice shook with fury and Serena alone understood that it was not just Pepper she referenced.

Serena put her arm around Pepper and guided her toward an empty guest room, firmly closing the door behind her. Tears came fast as she gathered the girl into her arms. "I'm so sorry! I thought he was downstairs but even so—it never should have happened! I never could have stopped him quickly enough and you should never had endured a single second of—"

Pepper pulled away, her tear streaked complexion mottled with the ravages of terror. "He got my skirts up but that was…he hadn't gotten round to the worst of it so you came in time, thank God! I…was so frightened! But you came in like an answer to my prayers and—" Pepper pressed her fingers against her lips. "Did you get him? I mean…like you said you would?"

Serena nodded, wishing she felt more relief. Even without the final act, the assault was no less repugnant to her senses. "Yes, it's over."

She put her hands on Pepper's shoulders and looked her friend squarely in the eyes. "You are *never* doing that again, Prudence."

Pepper smiled weakly, the first sign of her merry spirit returning to her. "Oh, well now I know you're serious, using *that* name."

"I mean it. The next time you offer to help, I'm going to lock you in a closet and ask the twins to stand guard." Serena touched her maid's cheeks, cradling her face in her hands. "How will I ever forgive myself for what I've done to you?"

Pepper sighed. "You did nothing and, besides," she leaned her head to one side to savor the contact between them, "I think you'll feel better once you get a good look in a mirror. I think you clearly got the worst of it, mistress."

"I don't care. Bruises heal."

Pepper was quiet for a moment, then blinked a few times. "Oh, the twins did you say? I think I'd like that!"

It made no sense but tears gave way to laughter and the women clung to each other, grateful to be alive and safe.

Chapter Nineteen

The doctor spoke to Phillip in the hallway outside of James'
bedroom, apparently unwilling to involve the 'delicate
sensibilities' of the women in the matter. "I've slowed the
bleeding and applied a poultice. It's a prick, or even a small stab
wound but…without seeing the weapon I cannot ascertain how
deep or what damage he might have sustained." The doctor
cleared his throat. "No one has found the source of it?"

Phillip shook his head. "The women were unarmed. A
quick search revealed nothing. Not even a pair of sewing
scissors."

"Well, he's certainly well enough for conversation and the
constable is eager to get to the bottom of things, so I shall give him
leave to do so."

"Thank you, Doctor Greene."

The man nodded solemnly. "It's a sordid business this."

"Sickening, sir."

Phillip waited outside the door to try to summon his own control. Fury hummed through him and the desire to stride through the door and murder James was palpable enough to make breathing a struggle.

There was no question of James' guilt in the attack. Caught in the act, the women's injuries and his own mumbled admission that "it was a weakness" of his. Pepper had been ice cold in her terror but he didn't think he would ever be able to forget the sight of Serena. Bloodied and bruised though eerily calm at James' feet, his fist pulled back to strike her again.

He'd have run into the room if Pepper hadn't thrown herself against him, hysterically crying for them to save her mistress. He had never felt so helpless and so numb with rage.

*No. That wasn't true. The sensation was eerily familiar though the circumstances were altogether different. No. No similarities at all. Except for—Raven Wells.*

Phillip closed his eyes as everything began to turn. He fought it the way a lunatic fights the invisible hands that pull at his skin. For there was nothing to doubt. James was guilty. The horrible scene was over.

Except a part of him couldn't stop looking at Serena and wondering what her part had truly been. He didn't want to fall into the trap of the past and lose her in a blind cloud of suspicion.

But there she'd been. Proud and calm in the middle of pure chaos, and Phillip's instincts sang in alarm. Lady Serena Wellcott had been in command where one least expected it and anyone who'd missed it was a fool.

*Enough. She is innocent and no one but James is to blame.*

Phillip returned inside James' bedroom, leaving the door open. James was sitting in bed like a petulant toddler.

"God, what an unthinkable fuss over a piece of tart!" James barked.

Phillip strode over to the bed, giving in to the icy fury filling his chest. He'd hauled his cousin's husband up by his nightshirt and began to shake him like a ragdoll before James realized his mistake. "You, worthless animal!"

James fought back weakly, blubbering. "Warrick! I…I am a gentleman! The maid swore she liked it rough and I was intrigued. I acted only to spare Delilah—a man's appetites are—I am...."

Phillip shoved him back on the bed in disgust then moved to yank on the bellpull. "Shut up, James! Stop talking or I swear to God, I will beat you senseless!"

The constable came quickly with two local strong men at his back. What Phillip didn't expect was to see Lady Serena Wellcott and Delilah also coming into the meeting. The bruise over Serena's eye had bloomed into a dark purple and her cheek was swollen but she was defiantly beautiful, holding his cousin's hand.

"Where is the maid in question?" the constable asked.

"She is resting in the blue bedroom. The doctor gave her a sleeping draught but if you need to question her, it can be arranged later," Serena said without emotion. "I am Lady Serena Wellcott, her mistress, and I was the one who interrupted the assault only to be...struck by Mr. Osborne."

"Let's not trouble the girl as yet but hear your side of it, Lady Wellcott."

A quick recounting of the morning's events was made and then Delilah added her voice to the fray. Phillip listened in amazed admiration at her courage.

"I have learned that this is not his first violent act in this house, Mr. Preston," Delilah said softly, her voice also level and strong. "My housekeeper made notes at my request to recall an accounting of the maids who have suffered and left our service as a result. I am sure those girls will testify to the worst of it."

"When did you ask her for these notes, Mrs. Osborne?" the constable asked.

"Just yesterday. Lady Wellcott's maid, Pepper, confided that she was afraid of my husband and I was inspired to make inquiries. I am ashamed my instincts were so slow to understand why we have lost so many young women from our service."

"Delilah!" James roared. "This is—a ridiculous conspiracy!"

Every eye turned toward him and it was clear that the only thing 'ridiculous' in the room was James Osborne clutching his bleeding bandaged balls and braying about his innocence.

"Here are Mrs. Watson's notes," Delilah held out a folded paper to the constable. "I am sad to say that I have read over them and can verify their accuracy… I fear it is a chilling and true accounting."

"Think of the scandal, Delilah!" James moaned. "What are you saying?"

Lady Wellcott sighed and stepped forward to touch her friend's shoulder. "He does have an unsettling point. The scandal will affect you all—even your unborn child, Mrs. Osborne."

Phillip gasped at the revelation, instantly gripped by joy and sadness for Delilah. *God, how long has she prayed for a child? And now to be faced with this mess?* But he was also set back on his heels at the unexpected twist of Serena cautioning against exposure. *Surely the best revenge is seeing James tarred and feathered for his assault?*

"What do you wish to do, Lady Wellcott? Mrs. Osborne?" the constable asked. "If he is charged with these crimes, it cannot be kept from the locals and from the papers."

"If I may," Serena spoke again, "perhaps now is the time to strike an agreement. I'd advised Mrs. Osborne that I would be amenable to a compromise but only if her husband agrees to it."

Delilah looked at her husband, her gentle shy spirit giving way to a woman infused with fury. "My husband will sign over the running of the house and holdings to me, he will leave this house shortly thereafter and he will leave England before the week is out. James has always had a fondness for the west."

"I will not be thrown out of my own house!" James protested.

"Then you can be hauled out and rot in prison or be shipped off to Australia in exile," Delilah countered calmly. "But make no mistake, James. You will *not* live here with me."

"Delilah!"

"I am sparing you a divorce only because I don't want to rob our child of his legacy and I am offering you your freedom, James. You will leave. Leave and never come back! If you do, then be aware that the constable will retain that record of your transgressions. Only prison and ruin will greet you if you return."

Phillip clenched his jaw but said nothing. He wasn't entirely sure that it would be legally binding, the notes of a housekeeper years after crimes had been committed or even the testimony of his victims if a judge refused to hear them, but it was clear that James had no sense of it to argue. *And of the recent attack, there's no question at all, and that's the noose he won't climb out of.*

"If you agree to everything immediately and sign the legal paperwork directly, then I am offering to send a small stipend to assist with your expenses." Delilah held up a hand before he could protest the word "small". "Fight me and I will give you *nothing*, not one penny."

"Delilah! I'm a man! Surely all this fuss over—"

Delilah turned to the constable. "The youngest girl on that list was twelve. These are not hardened women of the street. These were good girls who came to our service entrusted by their families to make better lives for themselves and—"

"Very well! Very well! I will…go."

Lady Wellcott took Delilah's arm. "We'll draw up the paperwork to ensure that Mrs. Osborne has her due and her child is acknowledged as the heir. Mr. Osborne can sign them before the sun sets."

"Mr. Preston," Delilah said to the constable. "Please. Stay until the papers are signed if you can and then see that Mr. Osborne is safely escorted to the mail coach."

"Yes, ma'am. With a glad heart," the constable said and the men retreated to the hallway.

"I'll meet you in the study downstairs," Serena said. "We can draft the agreement and have it ready by the time the solicitor arrives." She turned to Phillip. "Will you witness it when the time comes, Sir Warrick?"

He nodded. "If it protects Delilah..."

James growled from the bed. "Traitors and thieves! All of you!"

Phillip shook his head. "You'll leave with your reputation intact and a chance for a new life, James. It is more than you deserve, God help you."

*But why do I have the sinking feeling that you've only begun to pay for your sins, James. Because that was so much tidier and painless than—than Lady Serena Wellcott's gaze*

*promised when she was looking at you.*

*You, James, are screwed.*

Chapter Twenty

"That was…" Delilah sank into a chair by the fireplace and the women sat together to try to recover from the day's events. "I can't believe it is over."

"The constable left with him and they'll see him to the midnight mail coach." Serena watched the flames. "I saw him and I must say with vast satisfaction, James did not look well."

Delilah became very still before she whispered, "Did you poison him, Lady Wellcott?"

Serena smiled. "Not exactly." She shook her head and refocused on Mrs. Osborne. "But I think it is too soon to reveal the details. Why not savor your freedom and the relief of knowing that not another maid in this house need work in fear or dread walking the halls?"

"I am truly the mistress of Southgate Hall thanks to you, Lady Wellcott!" Delilah sat up a little straighter, a new light flooding her eyes. "Dell and I will travel abroad for my "confinement" and when we return, there will be a baby in this house, at long last! A baby to banish nightmares and bring happiness to us all!"

Serena laughed. "I think it is the perfect end to this tale!"

Delilah laughed as well but then sobered. "I am stronger than I look. You said as much, Lady Wellcott. Tell me. Tell me everything."

*So much for diverting her with talk of baby names…*

"Very well." Serena shifted in her chair and resumed the mantle of the Black Rose. "James is a rapist and while I knew I could remove him from the house, it was hard to ignore the greater picture. Any woman in his path would be in danger."

"Oh, god. You did poison him!"

Serena tipped her head to one side, absorbing that sweet, shy Delilah Osborne sounded less horrified than expected. *Even so…*

"I gelded him."

Delilah gasped, her fingers flying to her lips to cover a wicked smile before she blushed at her own daring. "That's—brilliant!"

"It is a bit grim but here," Serena said as she reached up to remove the entire hair pin and sheath from her hair. "See the jade carving? And the blade?"

"So cunning!" Delilah pulled the blade out but then stopped as she realized that it was still coated with her husband's blood. "Oh, god…it is a deadly thing, isn't it?"

"It is," Lady Wellcott agreed. "Every day, Pepper obtained fresh ingredients to taint the blade."

"Fresh ingredients?" Delilah asked, returning the weapon to Serena.

"From Dell's chamber pot." Serena closed the weapon with a soft *click* to safely set it back into the curls atop her head. "Revenge can be a messy business. But I used your maid's filth along with a few other things to guarantee that that one small puncture will cost him at the very least his sexual powers and if he refuses amputation when the infection sets in, potentially his life." Serena smoothed out her skirts. "But if he dies, it is by *his* choice."

"Like Lord L," Delilah whispered.

"Like Lord L." Serena stood. "Welcome to the Black Rose, Mrs. Osborne. I will naturally, stay in touch and will want to hear news of how you, Dell and your beautiful baby are faring."

Delilah also stood, her expression steady, her eyes clear. "I am forever in your debt, Lady Wellcott."

"Ah, the small price of membership," Serena said with a smile. "Tonight, I will leave as well."

"No! Please do not rush off!"

"If I have learned anything in the last few years, it is to anticipate when my departure is eminent." She kissed Delilah's cheeks. "We will see each other again. Don't fear."

Serena retreated without looking back and made her way upstairs.

There was no putting it off. She would have to face Phillip.

And she was determined to hold nothing back.

*Win or lose.*

Chapter Twenty-one

She knocked on his bedroom door, a woman resigned.

"Is he gone?" Phillip asked his voice rough with emotion as he pulled her into his room. He locked the door without a thought. "I still can't believe what happened."

"Can you not? Mr. James Osborne tried to rape my maid," she answered, the quiet in her tone a complete contradiction of the storm inside of her. "*My* Pepper. Did you know that she was with me in the orphanage? That I met her there? My precious girl?"

His brow furrowed. "My god, I can hardly credit it! He has always seemed so—"

"Do. Not. Defend. Him." Her hands clenched into fists so tightly she knew she'd drawn blood. "Make such a mistake at your own peril, Phillip. There is no question of his guilt, no smattering of doubt for you to quibble over his manly virtues." She took a step closer to Phillip, squaring up like a warrior for combat. "He tried to *rape* my maid and would have succeeded had I not come in the room!"

"I wasn't defending him. Can you not allow a person to be shocked to find that someone they've known for years has revealed themselves to be a criminal?" He crossed his arms, determined for her to see the irony of their argument. "I am not the enemy, woman."

"No." She pressed cool fingertips to her temples. "It has been—a difficult day. I never wished to see Pepper in danger and it has taken its toll on my peace of mind. Forgive me."

"What? What did you say? You never wished to see her in danger?" His expression changed slowly until his eyes glittered with anger. "Did you *knowingly* put your maid, your 'precious' Pepper, in danger, Serena? Is this part of some scheme?"

Guilt fueled her own furious response. "Truly? Are you so late to the party, Sir Warrick? Yes. Your cousin requested my aid with her rapacious troll of a husband after he attacked her lady's maid and I came. Yes. I blindly thought that it would be an easy matter and have learned that nothing is easy when someone you love is in harm's way! But let's get straight to the heart of the matter, shall we? If she had asked you, what would you have done? Would you have done better? Or would you have advised her to simply make sure her next lady's maid was less attractive and given Osborne a brotherly lecture on being more discreet with his affairs?"

"That is—unfair! I would have..." Phillip's words trailed off as he flailed on the horns of the dilemma. He knew as well as she that there was no simple path through the tangle of a maid who tried to accuse her employer of such a thing; that the legalities fell onto the man's side of the case, but it was difficult to accept it. "I don't know what I would have done. But I would not have slapped the man on the back and wished him well."

"That is comforting. I'm sure Delilah and the women of Southgate would have slept better at your raging commitment to justice." She folded her arms. "My hero."

"I'll be damned if I'm going to defend a hypothetical failure to do more in your imagination, woman!" He gently seized her upper arms. "You came here to stop him! You were plotting all along for his end!  Why not tell me as much?  Why lie to me when I repeatedly asked you what your true purpose was?"

"When?  When you were convinced I was a scorpion at your picnic?  When I had no confidence you wouldn't run to James and point out the danger?"  She shook her head.  "Even when we…when it seemed that there might be some hope for us to recover, my loyalty to Delilah made it impossible to tell you anything."

"Truly?"

"What?  Can you look me in the eyes and tell me that if I'd outlined my glorious plans to wrest the house and holdings from James' hands, catch him in the act of assaulting an innocent maid; you would have cheerfully just watched it unfold?"

He hesitated for the space of a breath but it was long enough to cost him.

Serena pulled away from his touch, her expression alight with disgust.  "Yes, of course!  No matter if he'd raped a dozen girls!  Heaven forbid his rights as a noble Englishman are violated!"

"You are putting words in my mouth! And I am not arguing for that waste of skin but you cannot play judge, jury and executioner. You cannot."

She laughed in a bitter mirthless melody. "I can because I dare to do whatever it takes to balance the scales."

"You've balanced nothing. You may have stopped him this once. What makes you think he won't just pounce on the next hapless girl in his employ?"

"Because the only thing he'll be able to mount will be a saddle." She brushed her hands on her skirts dismissively. "I neutered him."

"You—what?! How?"

"I stabbed him in the balls with my hair pin," Serena said archly.

"My god! I hardly think that's—"

"I stabbed him with my hair pin coated with the shit of a maid he had raped." Serena stood. "An infection is inevitable. If the man survives, I highly doubt he will possess his manly powers."

"And if he doesn't survive the infection?"

"Then the devil can sort him out when he arrives in Hell." She shrugged her shoulders. "I got the idea from a historical accounting of England's infamous long bowmen and archers. They used to defecate on the ground in front of themselves and then plant their arrows in a row, tip down, in the dirt before a battle. It ensured that any injury their enemies suffered, no matter how minor, would likely be mortal."

Phillip sat down, his knees betraying his shock. "What have you become?"

"I am the Black Rose."

Chapter Twenty-two

"What the hell is a Black Rose?"

She looked down at him and drank in the sensation of standing on a cliff's edge. And then she simply took a step out into empty air and accepted the fall. "I'm sure I've already described it to you, or perhaps just its origins? It is a secret organization privately referred to as the Black Rose Reading Society if and when we are forced to speak of it in male company. Rest assured, the women of the Black Rose do not sit in drawing rooms to discuss the latest novels. It is an organization founded for the sole purpose of securing revenge for women who need it."

"Founded by whom?"

"By me."

"Are there so many women in need of vigilantes wearing corsets?"

"You would be astonished at the numbers I have aided to date."

"Justice for wealthy women? How is that some kind of equitable move?"

"The Black Rose serves *any* woman who approaches us with a worthy cause. But then, I don't have to explain or justify a damn thing to you, Phillip Warrick! You don't like what you see? Then stop looking and be on your way!"

"I won't be on my way!" He stood to face her. "If it is so secret, why tell me of it now? Is this what you were hinting at before when you said you'd found your place helping others?"

"It is and you'll tell no one, Phillip." She smiled. "Because it's too fantastical really. Who would you tell? And what proof would you have beyond this private conversation? I'd deny it all and you'd look like a babbling idiot."

He shook his head. "This is not who you are—not at heart! I won't see you twist yourself into the feminine version of the demon that made you what you are! Trent was misguided! You must see it! You must see that I never meant to be the architect of a single moment's misery for you!"

"The Black Rose has nothing to do with you! The letter you shoved in my hands was a godsend. It was the revelation that set me in motion and brought me back to life, but I am not defined by that day; nor by Trent, nor by you. No man defines me! I knew the instant I read Trent's vile lies—I knew the true source of my misery and the extent of your role. You were as much his victim as I was, Phillip. And though I may have toyed with the notion of revenge against you, it is pointless."

"Then what was all of this? A seductive game to teach me some lesson?"

"Was it? Was that all it was to you?" She stretched her hand out to him. "A game?"

"I wonder if that isn't all you know. Games and schemes and revenge—this Black Rose nonsense!"

"Nonsense? Tread carefully, Warrick." Something in her retreated and an icy coil began to tighten inside her chest. "Do not think you can demean something I have built with my own two hands, not without a reckoning you will never forget."

"Do you—is murder on the menu, Lady Wellcott?"

"Only our members are free to ask such questions and you, *sir*, are decidedly not qualified to apply for entry."

"My God. End this, Serena. End this while you still can." He shook his head. "You are—better than this."

"You ask me what I've become?" She walked away from him then pulled out her fan with a flourish. "I became what you made me, Phillip."

"I had no hand in this. None."

Her breath caught in her throat and she reached up to touch her cheek as if he had struck her. "I—I became what you desired, my love!" She moved toward him, forcing herself away from the wounded woman she had almost crumbled into. "I was always, from the first moment I saw you, in a strange chase to be whatever it was that you desired, was I not? You achieved my virginity in a blaze of glory, did you not? But then you pronounced me a villain and tossed me into the mud, Phillip! Was there a different path for Raven Wells? Was I to marry another? Was I to lock myself away in a religious cupboard and pray for forgiveness? Or would you have preferred a different course? Should I have drowned myself in the nearest pond? Should I have remained broken and cursed?"

He reached for her but she eluded his grasp. "Serena!"

"No! You do not like what you see before you, Sir Warrick? I do not appeal?" Her gaze narrowed in contempt. "What a shame! For let me tell you exactly what kind of villainess I am. I am the kind of woman who refused to let your judgment condemn. I am the woman who refused to be destroyed because the man who vowed to love me for all time proved to be without a shred of honor. I am the woman who decided that if the world were made of games that I would be the mistress of a greater game! And while I could not save my own soul, I would do whatever it took to see that no other woman had to endure the humiliation and cruelty that I had suffered! And my crime when I was yet a child of seventeen, Phillip? I was powerless and naïve."

"Innocence isn't a crime."

Her head tipped up and she gave him one last glimpse of the irresistible allure of Lady Serena Wellcott in full bloom. "You mistake me for the female child that you destroyed on a country road and left kneeling in a mud puddle. You make yourself a fool when you invoke a past that you do not comprehend. I," she proclaimed as she shifted to rearrange her skirts, a goddess in silks, "am *exactly* what I was meant to become and *you* can stand aside. I have *no use* for you, Warrick."

She started to sail past him but he caught her wrist and forced her against him. He winced at the bruise on her cheek but kissed her all the same, with a blind hunger that demanded her return to reason, to his arms, to any chance they had for happiness. He kissed her and her mouth opened to him, the familiar taste of her so sweet, the response of her body to his so compelling that it brought tears to his eyes.

*So close. God, it's all so close!*

He reluctantly let her go, to look down into her face and search for the answers he so desperately needed to hear. "Serena, how do I reach you?"

"You already have. You alone have my heart, Phillip. You always had it. I never took it back. I never abandoned you but I also never asked you for so much as a scrap from your table. It is you who circled back, you who found me and you who carried me back into your bed." Tears slipped down her cheeks. "I am what I am."

"I—cannot escape you. How is that possible that no matter what you've done, I can't help but see the girl I once kissed in a gazebo?"

It was the wrong thing to say. An icy wash of loathing flooded her chest and she began to shift off the bed, retreating from his touch. "Ah! Then here is where I demonstrate what it means to truly love. I love you, Phillip Warrick. I love you so much that I will be the one to spare you the bitter disappointment that comes with the understanding that I am no longer the girl in that gazebo who believed that a single kiss from you was a prize."

"Raven! Don't be so quick to push against—"

"Do not call me that name without leave. I am Lady Serena Wellcott. I am a heartless witch who experiences mercy only when I am the one to dispense it." She shifted her skirts behind her, in a flourish that boded her flight. "I have given you your share. I have told you the truth of that day, indulged my desires in your arms, and we are at an end."

He winced at the words 'heartless witch' recognizing them instantly. "That's nonsense. Nothing ends. I love you."

"You? You love the girl in the gazebo."

"No. I love you, Lady Serena Wellcott."

She shook her head. "You don't and I can prove it."

"What proof do you have? What proof could you possibly offer, woman? I'm standing here before you and I know my own heart and mind. I love you! I love you past reason, past arguments, past everything that has happened and every confession we've wrung out of each other! So what is this proof to send me packing?"

*Don't look back. Let him go. Here, cut here...and run.*

"Very well. One more truth, my darling Warrick. One more painful truth and then I suggest you take your time and decide if you can truly love me as I am. For I will never apologize for my path or alter it to please you, Phillip. Never. So, hear what I am about to say and do not speak without thinking it through. For there is one more slice of punishment I fear you failed to anticipate."

"Let's hear it."

*Love you.*

*I love you enough to make you hate me.*

*Here's the blade.*

*Brace yourself, Phillip, because this is going to hurt.*

"The next time you take a woman's virginity and make love to her repeatedly over a fortnight, perhaps you should make sure she isn't carrying your child before you throw her into the hedges."

"Oh, my God…" Phillip's voice nearly failed him.

Air fled the room and she watched the fierce light in his eyes give way to pain and betrayal, horror and guilt. She walked past him as brutal shock held him in place. "I win, Phillip. I win."

\*\*

Their bags were packed before the chimes struck the quarter hour and her gilt carriage was loaded and ready just as she'd planned. Pepper said little, relieved to be gone from the house and any traces of James. Phillip came down the stairs of the house just as the skies opened up in a torrent of rain, moving to intercept them as quickly as he could but Serena cradled Pepper in her arms and signaled her driver to achieve London proper in record time.

"With all speed, your ladyship?"

"As if Satan himself were on your heels, sir."

*Or you were carrying his Mistress back to Hell.*


*Finis*

Made in the USA
Charleston, SC
27 November 2014